Se...

of My

Face

KAREN ARDIFF

NEW ISLAND

Copyright © 2007 Karen Ardiff
The Secret of My Face
First published 2007
by New Island
2 Brookside
Dundrum Road
Dublin 14

www.newisland.ie

ISBN   978-1-905494-43-9

British Library Cataloguing in Publication Data.
A CIP catalogue record for this book is available from the British Library.

Printed in the UK by Athenaeum Press Ltd., Gateshead, Tyne & Wear
Book design by Fidelma Slattery

10 9 8 7 6 5 4 3 2 1

For Willie Parsons — 'Bon Secure!'
And most especially,
For Ciarán Ardiff, with gratitude and love

One

When I woke up this morning I was different from how I usually am. I say that because when I tell you about it you will probably think me strange, or that everything in my life is significant and odd. That isn't so.

I have my routines. I don't think there is a person in Ireland who doesn't. You have to have a way of doing things in the morning because you are not yet quite woken up and if you didn't have a routine God knows what crazy things you would do. I am often thankful that I do things in a certain order and so avoid the pitfalls.

I always wake up before the others. It's no trouble to me at all; I don't even have to think about it. In summer the first light wakes me, and in winter I hear the birds tseeping or some such. It wakes me anyway and I slip into my clothes as quick as quick, and tiptoe downstairs and out the back door so that I can get on with gathering the turf and fetching the water.

This morning I didn't really wake up because I hadn't slept. I had tossed and turned in my bed so much that the sheets were twisted underneath me all costaways. For the life of me I don't know why, but when I sat up at first light, I stayed there for an age staring at the dust that waking up makes, like a child looking at soap bubbles. My heart was hammering like a drum and I had to breathe deeply to make it slow down.

I had to do a thing today that I had never done before. That, of course, was why I was so agitated and peculiar.

Liam had been sent to Egan's shop the day before to buy a paper of hairpins and a ribbon, and Daddy had told me that the picture of the Virgin Mary over my bed was pasted onto the back of a looking glass.

I suppose now that Mammy must have turned the looking glass around when I was little. It would be like her to make a virtue of it and turn the back of it into a lovely picture.

I hadn't known about it being really a looking glass turned round, and I didn't know what to think when Daddy told me it. He was looking into his newspaper when he said it, so I said nothing about it because I didn't know what to say, so I went to bed, but I didn't sleep.

One thing I've always loved is brushing my hair. I do it after washing my face and there are little sparks that happen when I do it and little snaps in the air. My hair gets light and it floats around my face, all the strands fluffing out and sticking together so that it's like wearing a hood almost. But this day when I did it my heart was going like a train. This day, because the young doctor was coming, I had to do the thing that I've never done before: I had to tie it up.

I pulled the hairpins off the paper and kept grabbing handfuls of my hair and winding them around in bunches the way I've seen women in Mass. But I couldn't know what way the hair was because I couldn't see it. At this time my heart was in my throat and I knew that I was nervous because I found it hard to breathe.

I decided that the only thing to do was to take all my courage and turn around the Virgin Mary and use the looking glass. I prayed to her as I turned her, and I can only think that she didn't hear me for the hammering in my chest, because the next thing was an awful thing. I had never used a looking glass before. Of course I knew about my face. Don't be silly, a person knows about the things that are wrong with them and you just get on with everything. Although I admit that the time I heard Uncle Morrie talk of the girl in Sligo who was nearly as old as me and still got made right, I got hot inside my cheeks and ears and full in myself, if I may so express it. I had great hopes of the young doctor because medical science can do wonders with the things that nature has messed up on. Having said all that, I am not the kind of person who looks for reasons to be miserable.

I sometimes catch a glimpse in a window. I am used to turning away from any sort of reflection but sometimes it's just not possible and you kind of see yourself, but I never saw myself full in a looking glass before.

I turned around the Virgin Mary and the looking glass looked back at me. I don't mind admitting that it was a shock. My mammy had said that when a hare crosses a woman with child, that child will be born with a harelip and that was what had happened with me, but I never understood before that a woman can look like a hare. I was shocked by how big my teeth looked. It seemed indecent somehow that so much of my private inside mouth should be open to everyone and not a thing I could do about it.

To be honest, it made me feel quite ill. I had a curious feeling when I looked at myself, like a thing rushed up inside me, right through the middle. I had to steel myself to pin my hair away from my face and to tie it up with the ribbon, and it wasn't easy to do because my hands were trembling.

I'll tell you a strange thing that I did then: when my hair was bunched up behind my head and the ribbon was tied in a bow I slammed my fist into the looking glass. I only chipped a little corner from it, thanks be to God, but it cut my hand and needless to say I was mortified by my moment of madness. I covered my mouth in horror and the blood ran down in a crooked line over my fingers, but the queerest thing of all was the next thing: with my hand over my mouth I was looking into my own eyes, as it were, for the first time. Big, pale eyes they are, with light lashes to them and you can almost not see the eyebrows either. All the colours in them are weak ones, like on our sycamore tree just when the leaves are about to fall off. Once my eyes stopped being so shocked and just looked back at me they were quite nice. That was a thought I'd never had before and it made them crinkle around the corners and shine wet and that made them even nicer.

I suppose I must have been goggling at my eyes for ages and it was a pleasant thing. I know this because when I came to my senses and remembered all the things I had to do before Liam and Daddy got up, my heart had to start thumping almost from scratch.

I had long since eaten and tidied my things away by the time I heard their footsteps above me, thumping around, but although you would hardly believe it I did not have their breakfast cooking when they climbed down the stairs to get it. It seemed to take an age before the sounds of their bare feet turned into the sounds of their feet in boots and all that time I just stood there like an eejit. As they started to come down a whitey sunshine blazed through the window over the sink and seemed to drown the room with light, so I moved to the corner where the only good patch of shadow was and I faced the wall. The blood hammering in my ears muffled the banging of their boots on the wooden treads, and my eyes got stuck staring at the cracks in the plaster wall and I could not look away from them.

They stopped at the foot of the stairs. They must have been looking at the empty table and the cooling hearth for I heard Daddy breathing out in a very vexed way, and although I was scared I couldn't move my eyes. I know it seems foolish, but I think there was some kind of enchantment in those cracks on the wall.

'Veronica.'

It was Liam who said it, of course. His voice is pleasing and gentle, with a smile in it even when his face is quite serious. Although he only said my name, there was a little lilt in it that told me plain as plain.

'Turn around. Don't be afraid.'

There's a great difference in being *able* to do a thing and *wanting* to do that thing. I didn't want to show Liam what I saw in the looking glass. Sure, Daddy had seen me from a tiny baby with no hair on my head at all. I could tell from his manner that he knew very well what I looked like under all my hair. But Liam was always fond of me, in his soft-hearted way, and as I turned to face him I was very sad that I would have to make him change.

I looked straight at him. It's odd, without my hair around my face, all the things I looked at that morning seemed hard somehow, like someone had drawn around everything with a black pencil. Liam stared back at me, but for once I couldn't tell what he was thinking. I suppose Daddy was staring at me too, but I couldn't honestly say for certain-sure, because at that moment I was only looking at Liam.

Now, I am the kind of person who likes to be 'one step ahead', generally speaking. If I hear a person shifting about in a chair, or see them picking up a bottle and looking into it, I like to be quick to get that person a fresh bottle, say, or ask them do they need a thing got. I know when a person is restless and needing something, or content and needing nothing, but when my brother and Daddy were staring at me that day, I found it hard to think of what should happen next because it seemed as if we would all be stuck standing there for ever. It was very curious, like we were all under the sea.

'Your mother wore her hair like that.'

It was Daddy who spoke. His voice sounded like a voice does when it hasn't yet been used: broken up and soft.

Before I knew what was happening, Daddy marched right out through the back door, and I came immediately to my senses. I was all flustered now, for he hadn't had any breakfast at all, not even tea. Liam was looking at the floor, and not at me any more, and I think he was feeling awkward, for he looked like a person whose arms are too long for them.

'What time is he coming?' said he, hoiking up the sleeves of his jumper.

I shrugged my shoulders, as much as to say, 'O, I don't know!'

But the truth was I knew very well, for Daddy had told me that Dr Geraghty would be here by ten-thirty at the latest. I didn't lie because I am an untruthful person. I certainly amn't! I didn't tell the truth to Liam because my face felt flat, like a plate, and now that I had seen it I didn't want to move it into word shapes in case that might make it look worse.

I didn't speak at all as I cooked Liam's breakfast. It was a comfortable kind of thing to do, to listen to the bacon sizzling on the pan, and to saw slices from the loaf and smell the tea. I did all these things as if I was alone, in a daydream almost, until a spit of bacon fat hitting my face brought me back to reality. It was just after eight o'clock when Liam pushed his plate from him and stood up from the table.

'Good luck, Ron,' he said, and he smiled at me when he said it.

I had to put my hand right up to my mouth, because I could not stop a giggle rising up in my throat. The varmint knows that whenever he calls me that I always get a picture in my head of Ron O'Rourke, who used to help at mass. One day he went through the whole of the Good Friday vigil with his white vestment tucked into the back of his trousers, and every one of us in that church will have to atone for ourselves on the last day for snorting like pigs in God's Holy Church.

I stood idle for a moment after he left, smiling under my hand and light of heart. I was glad to be alone again with so much to do, and I attacked the work with a great vigour. I raised so much dust with my broom that the room was like a bright night sky with hundreds of stars glinting in it!

I don't know how dust gets laid down so quickly. If a person were not clean in their habits it would be understandable, but for a person who sweeps and dusts every day it is mysterious and vexing.

It was only half past eight by the time I had done everything, and indeed I had done everything especially well for the day that was in it. I had the door open to air the house, and the day was so fine and bright that the outside seemed to be calling me to go and walk in it. I thought that I could gather some pretty things to put in a bowl on the table and so make the room nicer for Dr Geraghty to be in, so I could kill two birds with the one stone, so to speak. I wrapped a scarf around my head, carefully, so as not to disturb my pinned up hair and I covered my lower face against the cold.

As soon as I stepped into the yard, I noticed the dish for the Samhain-folk was upside down. I was naturally very concerned, but as I set it aright, I was relieved to find that there was only a teeny sup wetting the mud under it. It must have been close to empty already when somebody's foot kicked it from the back step, so thanks be to God they hadn't gone hungry. Now, I know some people think it is unseemly for a Roman Catholic to leave out food for the fairy folk, but I have heard something of the dangers and personally I wouldn't chance it. It has even been my fancy to 'experiment' with various kinds of food and drink to see which are best liked by the fairy folk that are abroad on the seven nights of Samhain, and you'd never guess what I turned up!

With the usual two bowls, one for food and one for drink, no matter what I put into them, my luck was only the teenchiest bit improved. It wouldn't be cast iron, say, that a blackberry pie wouldn't mysteriously singe in the oven for no good reason, or a mouse wouldn't infiltrate the larder and do its business in everything. One day, I had nothing left over by the evening for a food bowl, so I just left out a thick mix of Horlick's Malted food drink – the plain kind, obviously – and I went to bed in the horrors of dread. Well!

You'll think me a liar when I relate that I had as fortunate a day after as a person could hope for!

I have always followed this 'recipe' since and things have not been too bad, all things considered, so I was relieved to discover that they had fed before the dish got upset, given the day that was in it.

The trees that grow behind our house are of all sorts, and only the wooden fence that Liam made against the foxes separates them from the back of the yard. Whenever my work is done I like to climb the stile and walk among those trees for it's a thing I get pleasure from. You can go as far as you like or just a little way and you would hardly ever meet a person, for the woods go all the way up to nearly the top of Shannack Hill, and there's nothing there except flat rocks and stony tracks that look like they go to better hills with a view but they don't, they only break your heart and wreck your boots. Someone would have to start right down the bottom of the hills on the other side to come near us, and really, why would you bother?

Once in a blue moon I hear footsteps when I'm out walking and I leave the track and flatten against the tickly bark until they pass me, but it is only ever my father coming back down with the caught birds making a papery flappy noise against the bars of the cages. It's a torment to me that the best time for singing birds is when the nettles are at their worst.

When I'm hiding there, I pretend I am a high-wayman in a kerchief, with a pistol in my hand, stalking my next victim. I let on that the common-day birds in Daddy's cages are golden clockwork nightingales that I must steal for Princess Evelina to have in her boudoir. I press right up hard against the tree and I turn around real sly.

Woods are a great place for imagining in. You can dream while you're awake, and you can make the dreams do whatever you want and not the other way round. I don't care what anyone thinks, I don't believe there is a thing wrong with it, because I only ever go to the woods when I have done all my work.

Sometimes, when the spring comes, I pretend that the bluebells are a magic carpet. Any wish that a person makes when they are standing among them will come true. I wish for all kinds of peculiar things and they always become real right there in the woods.

Needless to say, these things only happen in my head. I have never heard that bluebells can really make wishes come true!

I knew, of course, that there wouldn't be any decent flowers about, as it was so late in the year. So I set my heart on getting some holly, if I could find some really nice stuff, or some Johnny McGrory if the birds had not got to it. I pulled up a few bunches of ragwort though, just in case I would have to make do. I find its yellow colour cheering, even if it is a poor, untidy sort of a flower.

The leaves were thick and deep and I had to lift my feet up high to walk in them so that it was like marching. Some crunched under my boots, and others were slippy and soft, and the wetness of them reached right over the tops of my boots and crept up my stockings like dishwater creeps up a cloth. They made a nice sight; little rusty beech leaves mixed in with every sort of green and scarlet and yellow. I had a mad notion that I would like to sweep up a big, damp armful of them and set them in a glass bowl on the table, where I could look at them all day.

I was idling there at the edge of the woods, clutching those dirty, yellow weeds in my two hands when a frightening thing happened. I heard the noise of a person deliberately clearing his throat just behind me and my heart jumped up my neck so suddenly I nearly choked on it.

'Miss Broderick?' said a voice.

I turned around, bringing my hand up to my mouth, even though my scarf was already there. A thin, black-haired man was standing in the middle of our yard, holding his hat in one hand and a large leather bag in the other. His eyes bulged behind his glasses and they made him look like a fish. I nodded my head, to let him know that I had heard him, but when he took a step towards me, it took all my courage not to turn around and run into the woods. I knew who he was. 'Dr John Geraghty,' he said cheerfully and he waggled the leather bag. I noticed that his eyes did not smile. He glanced about the yard in an uneasy sort of a way and seemed to be waiting for me to say something. After a little time his eyes flicked down to the weeds I was holding and he said in a jokey way, 'Are they for me?' His mouth was smiling again and the stems felt suddenly warm in my hand. I shook my head two or three times very quickly and I let them fall to the ground.

'O,' he said, 'I didn't mean...' But he didn't finish what he was saying and just stared at me instead. I wondered what it was that he didn't mean. His face was flushed, and there were triangles of red on his cheeks that made him look pinched and hungry. His hair was so black it was almost navy-blue, like a magpie's wing.

'I got no reply when I knocked at the front,' he said after a bit and I didn't like the way he kept looking at me from behind his glasses with his boiled gooseberry eyes. 'I thought, well, if there's no one in the house, maybe I'll go round the back and I might find someone there. And here you are!'

He spoke loudly, although I was near to him and I could not think what on earth to say to him. God forgive me, but I was suddenly angry with him for coming so early. Instead of being in the clean house with pretty berries on the table, we were in the muddy yard, strewn about with twigs and dirty leaves. All my careful planning had come to nothing. The doctor was supposed to speak with Daddy, but Daddy was not back yet and the two of us were all alone in the yard.

I wondered how long we could stand there with nothing to say and my face grew hot and uncomfortable and I felt foolish tears prickling behind my eyes. I did not want to show my mouth to this young man any more; he was staring enough as it was. A drop of water hit my face, and then another. Within moments the yard was alive with bouncing raindrops that made a loud noise as if loads of people were around us clapping and cheering. It got so wet so suddenly that there was nothing to be done but to run for the house.

Dr Geraghty ran awkwardly like a new colt, all legs. Before he was even halfway to the door, a terrible accident happened. His feet went right out from under him and he landed on his rear in the thickest part of the mud in the yard. He reached his hands out in front to steady himself and they stayed there in the air for a moment. His bag and his hat had landed in a puddle and he looked exactly as if he was driving a motor car with his things on the seat beside him.

I pressed my scarf against my mouth, but I could not stop the laughter that juddered up through my body. I turned my face away in the hope that he might not notice my convulsions. Then I heard the strangest whooping sound rising over the noise of the rain beating down on the muck and I turned around to find that he was laughing too. If anything, his high, hooting laughter made me even more hysterical and hot tears squeezed out of my screwed up eyes and mixed in with the rain on my face. Every time I looked over at him, I became more helpless. His head was thrown back with laughter and he kept slapping his hands into the mud and making it splash over himself with no regard for his clothes. I had never before heard a man braying like a jennet and it made me laugh more than I ever laughed in my life. He turned towards me and we laughed so hard that we stopped making any noise except wheezes. Then a sudden coldness about my head and face stopped my merriment dead. The wet scarf had fallen around my shoulders and I was exposed to him.

Well, I need hardly tell you that the fun stopped there and then! I pulled at the scarf to try and get it back up on my head, but what with being out of breath from the laughing and also kind of panicky, my hands were clumsy and the wool got caught on my coat buttons. Another thing was that I was watching Dr Geraghty to see what he was thinking, so I couldn't see what I was doing at first. When I saw that he was looking down at the wet ground and not at me at all, I looked down as well and paid proper attention to my jumbled up clothes, and in that way I was able to get myself decent again.

After I had settled myself, Dr Geraghty pulled himself up from the ground and stood in front of me with a smile on his face that went all the way up to his huge eyes. Curiously enough, I did not feel half as shook as I usually do when somebody looks full on my face for the first time. Of course I knew he was a Doctor and a Professional man, used to seeing all sorts of queer things, and I think, too, the 'laughing incident' must have softened me up. But the biggest difference was something else: when my scarf fell down, he had turned away from me, not as if he was disgusted, but as if he knew I wanted him to. Most people stay facing you, but their eyes look another place as if they wish they were anywhere else but stuck looking at you.

'Em ... shall we try for the house again?' he said. 'Before we have to swim for it?' he added, smiling, and I saw that the red blotches were on his cheeks again.

I nodded, smiling back at him under the damp wool, although he could not see it. He turned and picked his way through the mud and puddles as if he was dancing very badly. I followed behind him and every step I took made a squelching noise that you could hear over the drumming of the rain. When we got to the house, I closed the back door behind us.

We stood there for a moment getting our breath and dripping huge mucky drips onto the kitchen floor. I don't think either of us thought we should walk further into the kitchen when we were so grimy and so wet. It was as if both of us were trespassing in some giant's house, for Dr Geraghty did not belong there, and I felt as if I could not cross the floor unless he did, so we lingered inside the door.

I did not know what to do, for I obviously had no wish to take off my scarf again even though it was heavy with water. The young doctor was beginning to shiver, as I was myself, but I could not think what I could do about that.

If it was Liam coming in like a drowned cat, I would have packed him off upstairs to change into some dry things and stoked up the fire for him, but Dr Geraghty was not Liam. He was a perfect stranger in a clean house, with his hat and bag leaking water onto the floor

'Look, Miss Broderick,' said Dr Geraghty suddenly with a shiver in his voice, 'would there be a pair of old overalls about, or a—'

Just at that moment the back door came crashing open and Daddy marched past us, collar up and cap down over his eyes.

'Christ Jesus!' he said in a very loud voice. I was naturally mortified at the obscenity and I made a very hard noise in my throat and when Daddy wheeled around at me I jerked my head in the direction of the doctor.

'O,' he said, and he glared at Dr Geraghty, dripping all over his kitchen floor. 'Geraghty, is it?'

'The same,' said Dr Geraghty, and he must have been nervous, for he gave a little bob like a girl when he said it.

'You're early.'

'Yes … er … sorry about that …'

'What the hell happened to you?'

'Had a bit of a tumble outside,' he said, with a little giggle that stopped very suddenly.

Daddy said nothing and just stayed glaring at the doctor as if he couldn't decide whether or not to lamp him one.

'Ferocious day, isn't it, Mr Broderick?' said Dr Geraghty after a bit.

When Daddy still made no reply, the doctor just kept looking at him helplessly, and his mouth made a little wavy grin, like a dog who is afraid you are going to give it a root. I don't mind admitting that I felt sorry for him.

Eventually, Daddy pulled his cap back from his brow and made a kind of a grunting sound that I knew was a good sign. He walked over to the fireplace and stood to one side of it, looked at the floor and said, 'Skip up there child and get some dry things on you. And *you*,' he pointed at Dr Geraghty, who gave a little start, 'you'd better drop that overcoat where it is and warm your tail.'

I almost ran up the stairs, that way I would not drip so much water on the floor. It was a relief to get away from all the commotion downstairs. I could hear no sounds from downstairs. Either they were not saying anything or they were whispering so that I would not hear them. From the way Daddy had looked at Dr Geraghty I didn't think that they would be sharing secrets, so I didn't bother putting my ear to the floorboards as I would normally do if I was curious.

My things clung to me, and where I peeled them off the cold air made goose flesh of my skin. My plan had been to change into my good skirt and blouse before the doctor came, but now I worried about how it would look if I came down all dolled up.

It was so chilly it was very hard to think. I made a bundle of myself with my legs curled up to my chest, and wrapped my big towel around me, tucking it under my feet. I was shivering but I forced myself to breathe in and out as deep as I could. When I breathed out I could see my breath, and when I breathed in the cold air made my teeth hurt. Under the towel my skin started to warm up a little and it felt like my head was poking up out of a cosy tepee.

There is a picture in our church, The Church of the Holy Ghost, of the apostles and Our Blessed Lady with the tongues of fire sitting on top of their heads. Our Lady is standing up wearing a blue outfit made out of rugs, but the others are all wrapped in blankets and sitting on the floor, with nothing showing except their heads. I always thought it was silly to have the apostles sitting around in blankets, and I decided that the man who drew it must have been bad at doing hands and feet. But now I wondered if they had all just come in out of the rain like me.

A curious fancy struck me then: there I was sitting on the bed, taking my own sweet time, while two men waited at the bottom of the stairs for me to arrive. For a little minute I let myself pretend that they were lovelorn suitors and I a princess. I bunched my ermine stole closer around myself so that my milky skin would not get reddened in the bitter air. Then, on a sudden whim, I threw it to the floor with a big swing of my arm and before I had really thought about it, I pulled on my Sunday things, and that was that decision made.

There was still no talk coming up through the floorboards and with my clothes on there was really no reason to delay. It crossed my mind to check my hair in the looking glass but I decided against that in the end. At the top of the steps I stretched out my hands to hold each of the wooden banisters and I breathed in a big slow breath of air to help me get down into the room. Good clothes are generally stiffer than work clothes for they get used less and the material in them is thicker so I felt quite held up and taller than usual.

There is a special way of walking that makes it difficult for other people to know you are coming. You sort of peel your foot off the floor when you lift it up and you never bang it down *ever* but gently lay it down like it was a tiny kitten. I could see that Dr Geraghty and Daddy had not heard me coming down the stairs so I had to make a little cough and my face got warm when they turned around to me.

The leather bag was on the table now and a chair had been pulled out between it and the hearth.

'Will you sit here, Veronica? I'm just going to have a little look at you.'

I went over to the chair and sat down quite quickly, feeling very hot. My heart was in an uncomfortable place in my chest and seemed a little loud. It felt strange to sit there looking at the middle of his jacket where his tie tucked in behind the buttons, for he was standing right in front of me. The smell of his clothes was like a wet dog, but you could get a bit of the soap that had washed him as well.

Being so close to him troubled me. From side to side I could see nothing but the black suit with Dr Geraghty inside it. The more I breathed in the smell of him, the more confused I became. My legs were jittery and I wanted to cross them very much for they felt like they wanted to wander about. Most people are nervous when a doctor is going to look at them and when you are nervous you want something to happen right away so as to stop the waiting. I didn't know what I wanted to happen and when I felt his fingers underneath my chin it was a relief. He raised my head and I smelled his clothes all the way up until I was looking at his face.

I knew right then that I must close my eyes. I have seen calves lifting up their heads to suckle just after they are born when nobody has told them what to do and I suppose that people sometimes know what to do too. His fingers left my chin and my face stayed just where it was waiting for his next touch.

'I'm going to look at your mouth now, Veronica,' he said and a salty thing touched my tongue and made it pull back into me. My mouth opened and his finger ran around the good lip and it tickled and then he touched my teeth where my other lip should have been. All the parts of my mouth were tingling, especially the raggy part.

'I want you to open wide now,' he said and I heard Daddy making a big breathing noise and I remembered that he was in the room. I opened up wide and Dr Geraghty pushed his finger in and it went up the hole in the top of my mouth and I felt like I wanted to get sick.

'Nearly finished now,' I heard, and the voice was a calming one. The spit in my throat gurgled and it made my breathing in and out have a noise. I was afraid that I would cough up something or make a mess but I concentrated very hard and I stopped anything from happening.

'Good girl,' he said, and it was over.

When I heard a waiting noise in the room I knew that it was time to open my eyes and get back to normal. Even so, I must admit that I did not want to and I stayed with my head up in the air and my eyes closed for a moment. When I opened them Dr Geraghty's suit was gone and I had to rub my eyes like you do when you have just woken up. I looked around me and Daddy and the doctor were looking at me like they were wondering how I was.

There was nothing wrong with me, needless to say, so I put a face on me that said, 'O, don't mind me'.

Daddy asked a question then.

'Well?'

Dr Geraghty must have picked up his bag for it was in his hand and he said, 'Well ... that's all we need to see at the moment. If you'll walk me to my car?'

'Right,' said Daddy.

The doctor turned around to look at me and I felt strange for being in the chair sitting down but I could not move.

'Thank you, Veronica,' he said and his face was looking at me until just before they both disappeared out into the rain.

Two

It seems to me that everything can go along in a humdrum way for ages, but when one unusual thing happens it leaves the gate open behind it and mad things slip in. The very next day after Dr Geraghty's visit, I heard the name Molly Puddie for the first time.

The morning was pretty much back to normal and with my hair fluffed around my face again I felt much more like my old self. When Liam and Daddy came down for their breakfast, I am glad to say that there was breakfast sitting there on plates waiting for them. There was even an extra rasher for each of them because I had two over from not feeding Daddy the day before, and I slipped more tea into the pot too, so that it was nice and strong for them.

My eyes felt quite bright for I had not slept very well the night before. I was as curious as curious-pence to know what had passed between Daddy and the doctor, but of course I would not think of asking out of turn. Instead of sleeping I had lain awake with my eyes closed and had the kind of dreams where you make the things happen. They are not as mad as the ones you only remember when you wake up, where you fall asleep in a treble clef, say, or the cat asks you a question.

The only trouble was that I didn't stop imagining things when I got up, and I set the fire and swept the floor as if someone was looking on admiring.

After a last big slurp of tea, Daddy started patting his pockets like he was looking for something and then he took two small slips of paper out of his trousers and shoved them across the table to Liam.

'That's those,' he said, looking into his mug.

I stopped what I was doing and turned towards the table. Liam had gone pink and he slid the slips over to his plate and pushed them under the rim of it. He looked very warm and anguished, just like when he handed me the ribbon for my hair the day before, so I naturally wondered if the papers were some ladies' thing.

'She's expecting you at six,' said Daddy, as if that was the end of the matter, and he scraped back his chair, plunked on his cap and was gone, leaving the mystery behind him.

Liam pushed a frilly bit of egg around his plate and stared at it like it had made him cross. By this stage I was nearly bursting with curiosity so I stalked up to him and folded my arms in a pointed way. He looked up at me all innocent, so I cocked my head to one side like a man at a mart, to tease it out of him. He pretended not to notice me for a bit, but then he made a great giving-up sigh and said sadly, 'I'm to take a young lady to the Abbey Theatre tonight.'

Well! About thirty different thoughts started popping off inside my head at the same time. I knew right off the chalk that somebody else's hand was in it, for Liam isn't the sort of person who would cross the road to see a play, let alone go all that way on the train, without a push. But the queerest thought of all was the idea that he might have a sweetheart.

My brother is a very big person with arms and legs that are longer than his clothes. His face is not like mine, God forbid, but it is a workaday sort of face and not the face of a dashing suitor.

When you see him outside he looks perfect, for outside is the right size for him and when he slaps a cow's backside to get her into the byre, she is brawny like him and they both look grand. O, it's hard to say what I mean, but young ladies are more indoorsy, perching on the edges of chairs so as not to muss the lace on the back of them. Liam broke one of our chairs.

'Her name's Molly Puddie and you don't know her,' Liam shouted suddenly to the frilly bit of egg. 'It wasn't my idea, God knows, and there's no need for any more talk about it!' he concluded, still talking to the egg, and with that he jammed his cap on and followed Daddy out the door in a very bad-tempered way.

I was shocked to hear Liam give such a long speech and be so unreasonable, but as his footsteps disappeared the shock trickled away, because something curious was happening in my head that put everything else into the ha'penny place.

His words were having a most peculiar effect on me. I stood gawping like a fish and all I could think about was the name Molly Puddie.

'Molly Puddie, Molly Puddie, Molly Puddie,' went the words inside my head, like a tiny army marching about. At first a picture of a lovely girl flickered in my head like a ghost, but the words of her name soon snuffed her out. They began to sound like the nonsense women say to people's babies: 'O! Wussa wickle ickle doteen!'

Ridiculous pictures started crowding into my head. I fancied Liam was kissing a roundy plum pudding with holly on the top of it, then the picture changed and I could see a tiny, fat pig peeping out of his breast pocket and it was wearing a bright purple bow. All the time the words kept getting louder, but now they had the wrong beginnings and endings.

'Deemoll Leepudd, Deemoll Leepudd, Deemoll Leepudd …' over and over I heard them in my mind until I thought I would go mad. I wanted to stop hearing that stupid name but it just got louder and more mixed up.

'EEMOLEEP UD! EEMOLEEP UD! EEMOLEEP UD!'

Now the words were so loud and jerky that I could hear nothing else. A desperate panic rose inside me and I knew if I didn't stop the clatter I would go cracked, so I shook my head violently from side to side to rattle the name out of it and I slammed my hands down hard on the wood of the table and made a terrible noise.

'NNNNNGHNGHNGHN!'

Everything stopped.

I stayed as still as a statue and I didn't even breathe, for I was afraid that the slightest thing might make the words start up again in my head. I moved ever so slightly just to see, but there was nothing.

Shaking my head so hard had made stars happen and they fizzed just at the edges of my eyes. I felt little smarts of pain in my hands where they had banged the table and I moved my neck very carefully just to see if it was safe. No mad words started up. All I could hear were crackling noises from the hearth and Mammy's mystery bird in the yard, the one she could never see.

It took me a couple of moments to feel like myself again, and once I had calmed down a bit I realised what had just happened. It wouldn't have taken a great genius to work out that I had been taken over by a curse, and that same genius wouldn't have to think for long to know where that curse came from.

I ran to the back door, but when I looked out I already knew what I would see. The dish for the fairy folk was lying in two halves in the centre of the yard.

I suppose you'd expect that such a dreadful omen would make me feel worse, but it didn't. In a strange way it was a relief to know what had caused the lunacy that had frightened me so much. Still and all, the situation was very serious and I knew only one person who would know what to do. I bundled up the two pieces of the dish in a piece of cloth and I prepared to go to her.

Cass Carmody lives only a mile away from our house, but I never visit her except on a Cass Carmody day: Monday or Thursday. This day was a Wednesday and as I wrapped my muffler around me and buttoned up my coat, I wondered for the first time what she did on the days when I did not see her. I realised that it could be almost anything.

I was torn over the issue of the breakfast dishes, but I decided that this was an emergency and I left them on the table.

It was crisp and wintery. On one bend of the road every leaf and berry was bright and clear, and when you rounded the next all was dark, for the sun was straight in front and blinding.

I took a special route that I knew. It meant that you were going off the road and into some people's farms, but it was so close to the hedgerows that it didn't really count and it kept you from the danger of the roads.

A man got killed by a motor car on the stretch of road between our house and Shannack post office. Nobody ever found out who he was and afterwards I had lots of dreams about being the kind of person who could get lost and never missed. I suppose I'm very lucky because Daddy gets demented if I'm even a couple of minutes late home and he sends Liam out looking for me, but some people don't have anybody who cares about them. It must be a terrible thing and it has made me very afraid of motor cars, even though I would love to go in one.

In the spring and the summer and even into the autumn I love going on the inside of the hedges because I take the time to see what flowers are there and to look at them and how they are made. But this was the winter and there was almost nothing to look at except the corpses of old rusty sorrel, which never die and give me the creeps.

I was glad to get to Cass's, but then I always am.

Now, Cass is a very queer person. Daddy says she is a crone and unnatural with it. I don't think

Daddy likes her much, nor Liam neither, but Cass says it is like with cats and dogs. Men like dogs but they give very short shrift to cats, for they only do their own bidding and men like things they can boss. I know the things Cass says are wise, but I'm never sure if they are proper.

Actually, you don't really have to listen to everything she says, for often it doesn't have a beginning and it almost never has a proper ending. Mostly she has already started talking before she opens the front door, so I have lost the thread by the time I see her anyway. She wears most of her clothes at the same time, even in summer, but every day she puts them on differently so there is a lot to see as well as hear.

Cass is very old but her eyes are bright green. She was a big friend of Mammy's, and I think she likes me because of that, but she must have been much older than Mammy for she looks to me to be a hundred, even though she is pretty. She has white hair that springs around her face in curls. She must cut it without a looking glass for no two bits are the same length but it suits her. I used to think that she must have been a beautiful girl who was still lovely, but then I saw a picture of her when she was young and I saw that she was a plain, lanky girl who got beautiful. Her daughter in Dublin is dead plain too, but she shows no signs of turning into a swan though she must be near forty.

Everybody thinks that I go to Cass's to learn my letters and the other things I would be getting if I went to school, but the truth is that she just gives me the books and I do all that myself after I go to bed. Mostly on a Cass Carmody day I sit on her ormolu stool and watch her swaying around the house, chatting to me and to bits of the furniture and showing me things, or we go on walks and she tells me secret things about what flowers can do and which of the old stories are true and which ones are all my eye.

Cass doesn't know anything about lavender wax or getting out stains, but she cooks the kind of things that men don't like, where all the things come from the garden and look very interesting. The one place I don't mind eating is in Cass's house for she never seems to look at you much. She drinks a drink that she makes herself and it is a horrible green colour with bits in it, but it makes her happy and snoozey. Daddy gets quite annoyed after drink, but Cass gets very amusing and she snores even louder than a man.

Mostly what I love about going to Cass's is to look at all the things in her house and to listen to her talking. Her house and her head must be very alike for they're both stuffed with unusual things and you'd never be finished with either of them.

Most houses just look like somewhere that people live, but Cass's house looks like a thing that grew out of a mad seed. I suppose it's just an ordinary house with brick walls and a roof of slates on top, but it is what is stuck on it that makes it interesting.

There is moss on the roof: green moss and rusty moss and a flat moss that's bright yellow like mustard. On the trees and the walls are wooden things with lard-filled gourds hanging out of them to feed the birds, and on some of the window frames are roundy bells that make a noise in the wind. There are twiggy creepers all over the front of the house and round the door. They have white flowers on them in the summer that Cass says are not jasmine flowers, although I never said they were because I wouldn't know.

One of my favorite things is that she has stuck bits of coloured glass on some of the windows, like the gems in a pirate's hoard, and when the sun shines through them they make crazy light over everything.

As I came up the front path I noticed that she had stuck apple halves onto spikes of an old dead bush. In my imagination, they looked like the severed heads of French aristocrats set on lances outside the town, but they were probably for some bird as Cass is mad for birds.

I was a little nervous knocking on the door for I never, ever call on someone when they are not expecting me, but then I remembered that Cass never seems to expect me even though I come at the same time every Monday and Thursday and am as regular as the clock.

The door moved slightly when I tapped on it and I realised that it was open. All the winter cold was getting in, but then Cass's house is always chilly, which is probably why she wears so many clothes. I knocked again, very gently, which opened it a little bit more. I could hear no sound of Cass but I could see all the way through the hall to the kitchen at the end of it.

The house looked strange, all still, with the hard, bright sunshine falling on the heaped up books by the walls. Through the window at the back of the kitchen I could just make her out, kneeling on the ground. I tiptoed down the hall and through the kitchen, feeling like a sneak thief.

I watched her turn over the muck with a little trowel and stick her hand in the hole it made, squinting up to the sky and fingering something in the ground. In the summer, I often found her at just that spot, stripping the leaves off dandelions until the wicker basket beside her was full, and the strange thing was that all her dandelions grew in the same place.

There were no dandelions there now that I could see. They must have been under the earth though, waiting to grow.

She was singing a song that sounded as if she had made it up herself and the only word I could hear clearly was 'Kan-ga-rooo' and then 'rooo, rooo, rooo'.

I watched her mouth puckering around the 'oooo' sound. When a person gets old they have lines that a young person only has when they make a kiss, and looking at Cass singing her song filled my head with thoughts of kissing mouths because her 'oooo' made her kiss-lines deeper. All of a sudden I wanted my mouth to make a kiss and my lips tried to do it but only my good lip would pull in.

That was how I was when, unexpectedly, she whipped around and fixed her eyes on me as if she knew I was there all along.

'Well!' she said, with a look on her like a cat that's just heard a scuttle under the floorboards. 'What's sneaked into your little cupboard, I wonder?'

The sharp curiousness in her expression made me feel uncomfortable. She seemed to know that something was wrong, so for an explanation I emptied the cloth bundle onto the grass between us.

She looked at the broken bowl for a moment, then she looked back up and stared at me as though she was drinking me in, and a rogueish look crept over her old face.

'No!' said she, with a sly smile. 'I don't think the fairies are the problem at all, lamb child! Or should I say *woman child*?' And she threw her head back and laughed a long, raucous laugh.

'You poor creathur!' she shrieked. 'I wonder now just what makes you feel *cursed* precisely?'

When I made no answer, she put on a makey-up scary voice and hissed, 'Bad, fierce, *wicked* thoughts, I sincerely hope! Well, get used to them cub, they're only going to get worse! More *detail*, d'ye see!' And she laughed again, long and hard, delighted with herself. I just stood there, gawping at her.

'Well, do you know,' she said when her laughing got less, 'I think we might have a bit of a celebration, you and me.'

I had no idea what she was talking about, but with Cass I often don't, so I kind of smiled with my eyes. She was being so light-hearted and merry that my fear started to leave me and my chest started to feel a bit less thumpy. Cass was still talking.

'God, I thought nothing would ever filter into that gloomy old cave down there with the two of them traipsing mud into the place and parking their arses down for food and not a word for a cat. Not even so much as a cat, now I come to think of it. Probably too much female energy for them even in an old tom, they couldn't handle it. Well! We'll have to sacrifice a fine cock to Old Ma Nature; she snuck in anyway. Right, let's get you corrupted. Follow me, woman child!'

She hauled herself up off the ground, making an elderly noise, and she stalked past me into the kitchen. I couldn't think what on earth to say to her, so I just trotted in after her like a good little doggy and kept listening.

'Early enough yet, mind you, even for me. Nine or something, is it? Still and all, making up the excuses is always one of the fun parts.'

'Actually,' she said, disappearing into the pantry where her voice got a bit muffled so she had to shout.

'*That's one of the rules: if you don't have a good reason, have a good excuse ...*' She reappeared carrying a bottle of her green drink and two glasses.

'GOT IT!' she said, still shouting, until she remembered that she was right beside me.

'Sorry ... I have it. It's only nine-ish, *but!*' and she stopped dramatically, holding the bottle aloft and keeping me in suspense,

'The sun is officially *fourteen years* over the yardarm! Sure you couldn't wait a minute more than *that* for a drink, couldn't you not?' and she laughed her head off again, thrilled with herself, and slammed the bottle and glasses onto the table. I wondered if she had lost her marbles.

'*Sit!*' she said kind of savage, but with a smile, so I sat myself down on one of her wooden kitchen chairs.

I was completely bewildered as Cass poured the cloudy liquid into the two glasses and handed one of them to me. Bits of green stuff floated around on the top of it and I thought it looked revolting, but Cass said: '*Bon secure!*'

I didn't know what to do but I felt excited, for no one had ever offered me drink. It didn't seem polite to not drink so I shook my hair in front of my face a little and I raised the glass to my lips. Cass was looking at me and had an expression on her face that I couldn't quite make out; it was a bit like a fox looking at a fat chicken, but in a nice way.

I have seen other people drinking and they close their whole lips over the glass and make a very small hole for the drink to go in. Whenever I drink tea I have to pour it into my mouth and suck it around my tongue, for my lips will not close. In the normal run of things I will never drink a thing when someone else is there, but this felt different. It felt more like mass or something.

I poured a little of the green drink around the underneath of my tongue. The back of my mouth closed slightly in a little cough, for as soon as it touched me the drink sent vapour into my whole mouth and right up into the hole in the top of it.

Once, I snorted tea up my nose when I was drinking and a funny thought came into my head and I laughed. The whole of my face felt uncomfortable and sore for ages and that was a little like how I felt now, but there was something else. The drink tasted like old leaves in petrol at first, but after a couple of pourings, as it slid around my tongue and burned down my throat, it tasted like dreams I have had of underneath the sea.

I wasn't able to put another pouring into my mouth because Cass's hand was suddenly covering the top of the glass. I realised that my eyes were closed because I opened them.

'Dizzy?' she asked. I was. I let out a breath that felt like you could see it. My whole head slumped down towards the table but it immediately snapped back up and these words came out of my mouth: 'Molly Puddie.'

I couldn't believe I had spoken. I pulled my hair away from my mouth with my two hands and I leaned on them, holding my face up in a big smile. My eyes felt very twinkly and I looked brazenly at Cass, who was swimming in the air in front of me. She wiggled into view and her features got like milk mixing with tea and becoming beige.

'Ah ...' she said, 'La Pudd!' She whooped a big white sound. 'Well ... what of?' she asked.

I could think of nothing else to say as I was feeling rather strange, so the easiest thing to do was to show her. I had put the tickets into my pocket so I just took them out and pushed them into the centre of the table like a conjurer.

Cass picked one up and squinted at the words on it, then she raised one eyebrow and said, 'Well! She's finally got him to bring her to somewhere swanky ... or so she probably thinks. I suppose the poor little muckeen expects that he'll just transform himself into a magnificent specimen of a gallant lover and his lunkiness will evaporate like fairy mist.'

She made a ripply movement with her fingers and laughed a little tinkly laugh that sounded a bit mean at the end.

'It'll be entertaining at any rate to see what costume she'll stretch around her hams for the occasion ... Of course the mother will probably

wheedle some readies out of Muck Pére for a fist-
ful of egret feathers or something to stick into
some bit of her … God and James's Street! The
mind boggles! I've always thought myself that girls
like that should be made to wear a uniform to
spare the rest of us from having to look at the
results of their efforts. Do you know, now that I
think of it, it was La Puddie's holy communion
rigout that started me on that idea actually,
because I was standing beside Brigid's first born –
the exalted grandchildette – for the whole thing
and I had to actually witness the lump's lace and
broderie ong-glaze collar absorbing snot from her
tap of a nose for the entire performance … I
nearly left my dinner in the bottom of the bowl at
FitzGerald's hotel for thinking about it afterwards.'

Cass said most of this to the air over my head,
and some of it to the tickets in her hand. I suppose
my eyes must have been out on stalks because now
I knew that Liam had been stepping out for a while
and I had known nothing about it. I wanted to ask
her all about it, but the thing with Cass is that she
doesn't have an expression that tells you she's about
to stop talking. With everybody else you can see a
gap coming up and you can be working out what
you want to say so as to have it all ready.

'And what passion-inducing spectacle has the
lovely Liam selected for his bovine love, I wonder?'
Cass went on, peering at the tickets and holding
them close up to her face.

'O, good Mother Earth!' she said, slapping them back onto the table and giving a loud hoot of a laugh. '*The Gods of the Mountain* by Lord Dunsany ... O, well that's just the most glorious thing yet! O, Lord Dunsany, Lord Dunsany, whoever you are, you're owed a big kiss. Sure they might as well knock the whole audience out with ether. I *betcha* it's five hours long, at the least. *Poor* Liameen. O! Don't you just want to transmogrify yourself into a head louse or something, Veron, so you could just be in the Abbey Theatre for the whole wonderful, gruelling night?'

I didn't want to transmogrify myself into a head louse at all, but you don't have to take what Cass says seriously, because if you did you would probably get into a lot of trouble and you would have to be a witch anyway.

I was beginning to get frustrated for she hadn't taken my meaning at all. I wanted to ask her about the madness that had come over me earlier and not to talk about my brother and his sweetheart. I didn't want to think about the two of them together and what she might be wearing on her skin, but my tongue did not feel as loose as it had before.

Cass was looking at me with a questioning look, but I had already forgotten what question she had asked me. All that had happened since yesterday was getting muddled and I didn't feel like myself. Cass started talking again but I couldn't hear her, only muffled noise. I reached out for the glass in front of me and took another suck of the cloudy wine. The vapours filled all the parts of my face and the liquid burned as it trickled down my throat. At the very last moment my swallow reached up and grabbed it down deep into me.

I closed my eyes and felt a heavy ache behind them, like sleep, and I felt things: I smelled soap and wet cloth, and my heart made a strange sound inside me, like when your ears are underwater and you knock against the bathtub. Butterflies were dancing under my chin and they lifted it up so I could feel light shining on my face. My lips came together in a kiss and both parts of them closed around the tiniest, most perfect hole. The kiss closed more until every part of my lips was touching every other part and the next thing would surely be the beautiful noise.

I came to my senses rudely as air whistled over my teeth through my raggy lip and made me wince. I felt two hands covering mine and I saw Cass's face very close to mine and she looked disturbed. She said nothing, which was very unusual for her, and she squeezed my hands tightly. I don't know what happened, but a big welling of tears rushed up behind my cheeks and spilled out of my eyes and I lost all control of myself.

Cass kept a hold of my hands so I wasn't able to rub my eyes or cover my face. The sobs were hacking up from my chest like coughs but I didn't even try to stop them. The relief of it made me almost laugh under the tears, for it was like finding something you have turned the house upside down looking for. I realise now that I must have been very affected by the green wine, for I found that my body liked the convulsing that my strange crying fit made happen. It was exciting.

When my body got too tired to keep up I would be silent for a moment; then my breath would snatch into me violently and the sound was heartrending, even to me. I could not stop.

I have just told a lie. I did stop. What I meant is that I felt that I would never stop, but what seems true at one moment is a lie the moment after. I always thought that a person is just who they are and nothing ever changes, but perhaps we are like a chain of dolls cut out of newspaper: they are all the same shape, but where one ends another one begins, and though they are cut out with the one scissors they have different words written on them.

My eyes were hurting now and I looked up at Cass and slipped my hands out from hers. I was not sure what way my hair was but I was too weary to check. I could feel a wet strand of it over my cheek but I didn't care if it was covering my mouth or not.

'I'm a careless old bitch,' she said quietly. I didn't think anything of the obscenity for I wasn't thinking much at all.

'God, Ellen sat just where you're sitting with the same red eyes and leaked milk for thinking of you and what this day would do to you.' Ellen was Mammy's name. What day? I thought.

'She couldn't feed you. Did you know that?'

I stared at her.

'You couldn't suck. She fed you from the old yellow cow that your father made so much of: Evelina. Evelina's milk in little bottles, with teats of rubber that made your mother so sad. She used to run her fingers over them and then touch herself where she couldn't get in deep enough to get her good milk into you. I told her that you'd thrive, that you had that look about you, but she wanted to give you strength herself. She loved you so much, Veronica.'

I got up from the table and I walked down the hall and left her sitting there.

My hands were out in front of me like a blind man's and I hit one of the hall walls with my palm as I left. Now that I think of it I was not like a blind man, but like a drunk.

I followed the road and not my normal path. Once a motor car swerved into the middle of the road to avoid me but I wasn't frightened. I was walking, I suppose, but it felt as if all the way home I was stopping myself from falling. My head was leading the rest of my body, which followed in a zig-zag path until I came to my own home. I climbed up to my room with my hands three stairs above my feet, crawling. I fell onto my bed and slept in my coat.

Three

Even though my eyes were closed I knew that it was still day. I used to think that eyelids must be see-through, but in fact it is inside that you sense the difference between day and night. The dark presses down on a face, but light makes your head fill up with an invisible something until you have to open your eyes to let it out.

Usually I find this a pleasant thing, but this time the invisible something grew so large that it hurt my head, and under my eyelids seemed white hot. I could not think where I was. Then I heard a sudden movement and a hand pressed against my forehead. I knew it was him because I could smell him.

'*Christ, Christ, Christ.*' My father's voice came from across the room. I opened my eyes and my head squeezed in around them and they hurt. Normally, when I open my eyes they work straight away, but this time I saw blurry shapes that only slowly showed themselves to me as what they really were.

Dr Geraghty was leaning over me, and behind him, by the wall, Daddy and Liam were staring. I tried to lift my head but it felt like lead and a great heave of sickness rose up inside me.

'No, no, Veronica,' said Dr Geraghty. 'Lie still.' He kneaded my forehead with his hand, like a weight of darkness driving out the light.

I closed my eyes and they slipped away from me.

❖

When I woke next it was dark.

I was hot and the bedclothes clung to me where my skin was touching them. I lay there for a moment and waves of something moved through me, so I just let them, until there was a kind of stillness in me. I turned around on the pillow without lifting my head, and then I pulled myself right out over to the edge of the bed and slid out onto the cool floor like an eel.

I was sleepier than I had ever been before, and although I couldn't recall what had happened, I wasn't frightened, just numb.

I heard voices from the room below, and because I could not move I listened. I have often lain on my bedroom floor, listening when Morrie and Kitty are there, or some other visitor, and it is better even than a wireless. The boards were so smooth and my mind so still that the words went into me as if I was having a dream.

'You will go!' Daddy was shouting.

'I'll not go while she's lying there ailing.' Liam spoke quietly and my heart gave a leap for I knew he must be speaking of me.

'She's not ailing. She's *heartsick*.'

There was a silence after Daddy said this. There was no energy in me for a swallow so the drool from my mouth trickled out to the floor. I had almost forgotten that I was listening for anything at all by the time he spoke again.

'They're all so fucking ... They'd have had me parade her in the streets in front of everyone or stick a knife in her and make it all go away, not a loss on them.' His voice was tight and high, as if it hurt him to speak. It was peculiar to hear him talk so late without slurring. Liam said nothing at all. He must have been listening, though, just like me.

'I've had my heart in my mouth all these years every time your uncle graced us with a visit. I knew the little sparrow-fart would say it in front of her in the end. "*If it's the money, Dom ...*"'

Daddy did a put-on voice that sounded mincing and vicious. I heard Liam's voice now, cutting across him.

'He's only trying to help ...'

'He's not trying to help, you ignorant little bollix! He doesn't want to have to look at her! It offends him that there's something broken in the family. He wants it ... *fixed.*' Daddy was shouting now. 'Didn't you see her? She's falling asunder. That lanky bastard laid his hands on her and filled her with hope. Jesus Christ, man, she practically shut down with panic when the new money came out! How the hell is she supposed to cope with this? They just want to sew her up and move on to their next little project; they don't know her, they don't know what a child she is.'

The room went quiet for a while. I heard one sound that sounded like a sobbing noise, but it was so quick that I might have been mistaken, then Daddy spoke again.

'I'm going for a drink.'

'I'll wait with her.' Liam had barely said this when Daddy interrupted in a slow, tight voice.

'You keep your appointment, d'you understand me, boy? Every plan I've made is not going to ruin over this. There's more than just land at stake here and you'll do no better, so don't you think you will.'

I knew from the tone of his voice that whatever happened next would be important. Nobody made a noise for a moment and then I heard the scrape and crashing down of a chair and one of them stomped over to the door and banged it after him. Although I could not see him I knew that it was

Liam, because Daddy would never have left without being answered.

I stayed lying on the cold floor for a while longer until I heard a second person slamming the back door behind him and I knew that Daddy had gone down to Tubridy's to drink stout and give out about the way Ireland is going.

It is a curious thing to hear yourself mentioned in a conversation when you aren't supposed to be listening at all. I did not understand all that Daddy had said but I was disturbed inside by it nonetheless. It was strange to hear him talking about why I was feeling sick and getting it all wrong, but I was relieved that he hadn't guessed about Cass's wine.

Now that I had time to think of it, there was a thing that made me feel almost angry. Daddy had kept the doctors from me all those years. He hadn't wanted me to be fixed, but I wanted to be fixed. And it wasn't my fault I got upset about the money. I was just used to the old money was all, and I always think the beautiful lady on the notes is staring at me. That was a terribly unfair thing for him to say.

I thought about Uncle Morrie. He saw that I was broken and he wanted to do something about it. He was the one who had brought Dr Geraghty to our yard and not Daddy at all.

I felt different inside after I had thought of these things and my tiredness kind of lifted. I raised myself up off the freezing boards and I knew I wanted to do something, but I wasn't sure quite what. I was still in my coat.

I decided to go downstairs and I didn't bother going quietly because there was no one in. At the bottom of the stairs I stopped to look around. My scarf was lying over the kitchen table where I must have taken it off when I got back from Cass's. It was lying on the dishes that they had eaten their breakfast from and it must surely be dirty.

The room looked dreadful. There were more mugs than just the breakfast ones and whoever set the fire had let ash and crumbled off bits of turf fall on the floor. I could not understand why they had not cleaned it up as they thought I was ill and couldn't. That is to say Liam thought I was ill; Daddy thought I was heartsick. I suppose a person who is heartsick is still able to clean a house when everyone else has gone out to the pub or the theatre.

A sudden thought came into my head and my chest gave a bang. I shoved my hand into the pocket of my coat and I didn't even have to take them out to feel that they were there: the tickets.

I felt hot all of a sudden even though the fire had died down in the room and it was chilly. I couldn't move for a moment and my brain wouldn't think for me. I held on to the banister and I tried to breathe in and out more slowly. I couldn't think how I might get the tickets to Liam and stop the whole night being ruined. He was surely on his way to the Puddie house now to call for his sweetheart.

If I followed him there I would have to show myself and shame him. After all, a young man on a romantic evening doesn't want his little sister turning up and putting a spanner in the works, and anyway, I didn't know where the Puddie house was. Then another thought struck me. Surely Liam must know that the tickets were not in his pocket. If he did then he was not just trying to mind me by telling Daddy he would stay at home. Maybe he was trying to get out of a hole.

I sort of rolled this idea around in my head and I must admit that I enjoyed getting myself worked up about it. I am not normally a person who gets vexed, and as Cass says a change is as good as a coort.

In the end, though, I decided that Liam isn't that smart of a person to work out such a devious plan. When I was trying to think of him being mean I kept seeing him in my head and I couldn't make him do mean faces, even imaginary ones.

Time was against me. Liam must have been gone nearly half an hour and since I didn't know exactly where his beloved lived I didn't know how long it would take him to get there. She didn't live very near, though, for I knew everyone who lived around Shannack and I didn't know her.

As I started to form my plan I got excited. Up until this morning I had never left the house on my own without Daddy knowing where I was going and now I was going to do it twice in the one day.

What I decided to do was to go to the station and leave the tickets there. In books I have read, some of the most interesting things are done 'anonymously', so I wrote 'LIAM BRODERICK' on the back of the tickets in capital letters, and no one who knew me would have known it was my writing, for I took care to change it.

As I had been in my coat for a whole day by now I didn't think I would feel the good of it, so I grabbed Daddy's old wrecked coat that he wears when he's capturing birds and I put it on over my own. It smelled very funny and there were gluey patches on it from the stuff he puts on teasels to make the song-birds stick to them, but it felt like a disguise.

I was thinking very quickly now. I knew that Liam would be the one to buy the train tickets, for he was taking Miss Puddie out and a lady never puts her hand in her pocket when she is being courted. If I could put the Abbey tickets by the counter she might never need to know that he was a featherbrain.

I picked up my scarf to wrap it around my head, but it was soiled with egg yolk and one end of it was in a cup of tea, which had seeped up the wool and soaked it. So I took Liam's cap from its nail; he must have been wearing his good hat. I pulled a clean dishcloth from beside the sink and I tucked one end under the cap at my left ear and the other end under the cap at my right ear. I was all set.

I stepped out into the dark night and my heart was thumping with the strangeness of it all. The night was cold and my breath came out through the dishcloth like steam from a kettle. It was quite a long way to the station and I imagined to myself that I was a mercenary soldier on a secret assignment and I kept very far from the road so that I was almost walking on the edge of the ditch. I didn't go into fields like I usually do for I had no time. Once or twice I heard horses' hooves and now and then a motor car, but every time I flattened myself against the damp hedges and pretended I was hiding from the Boshe.

The wind got stronger and it filled up my head with noise, and when it started to rain my body started to shiver under the big coat. But a soldier doesn't complain about a silly thing like the cold, even a mercenary one.

I slowed down as I reached the station, feeling all sneaky, like a cat. The light from inside spilled right out onto the road and I wasn't that keen to step into it, so I snuck up sideways to the door. I pulled my cap down on my head and lowered my chin to my chest, for it occurred to me that the dishcloth might look odd. I went inside very cautiously, letting on to be a short man who was looking interestedly at the floor. I was terribly excited and nervous.

There was a man in the ticket office and he was reading a newspaper. I hadn't ever seen him before as I had never needed to get the train, but he looked to me to be a grumpy sort of a person. He kept his mouth closed when he blew out his breath and it made a sound like this: 'pppppppph', and when he breathed in again it was like snoring. He didn't look like the kind of person who would like to be disturbed by someone who wasn't going on the train, so I looked around to see where I might leave the tickets. If I was very clever I wouldn't have to let him know I was there at all.

The station was empty as the next train wasn't due for quite a while, so I crept over to the booth, hugging the wall. I knew I had to be quick: it would be a disaster if Liam and his sweetheart were to arrive before I had completed my mission. I didn't know how much time I had.

I noticed that there was a sign in the bottom corner of the glass that had all the train times on it. That was just the cover I needed. I stood to one side of the window where the man could not see me and I slid the two tickets across the shelf. I propped them up against the part of the glass that had the sign on it, with the writing on them facing out. I waited a moment to see if he had spotted anything, but he just kept breathing out 'ppppppph' and making his newspaper rustle.

I started to tiptoe out of the station at double time, as if I had just set an explosive and had to get far away before it went off. Just as I got to the door I heard a woman's voice outside saying Liam's name and I froze to the spot. They were here.

I looked around me. There wasn't a single place I could hide except behind the door. I got there just in time, for no sooner had I wedged myself in than I felt a shove against me. Someone had banged the door and they were coming in. I heard a loud voice saying, '*Liam Broderick!* Listen to me when I'm talking to you! I swear if you stand about tonight like an Egyptian mummy I'll absolutely scream!'

Then I heard my brother say, 'Sorry, Molly.'

He said in a quiet way that made me know he did not want to be talking at all. There was a tiny breath of a gap, and then the loud voice leaped in again.

'Open your beak and speak! Sacred Heart, it's like walking out with a dumb animal! I swear half the time I wouldn't bother seeing you if my mother wasn't so keen. You're only *this* side of simple!'

The woman spoke with a strangled voice, as if she was pushing something heavy up a hill, but I knew it was anger that made her sound like that. I stood in the dark behind the door and I hardly dared to breathe. If Liam didn't see the tickets it was likely that this Molly Puddie would run him through with a hatpin outside the Abbey Theatre.

A big, deep sigh on the other side of the door told me that Miss Puddie was right beside me although she didn't know it. She was making so many sighs that I could tell they were not real ones and only to show Liam that she was still annoyed. Through her noises I could just hear Liam saying to the ticket man that he wanted two return tickets to Dublin, and the ticket man said 'One and six' in a gruff voice that sounded as grumpy as he looked.

Molly Puddie began to drum her fingers on the wooden door. She must have had quite strong hands, for the noise was very loud to a person whose ear was only an inch away. It made it hard for me to hear Liam, but I could just make out that he was talking more to the cranky man. Then I heard the man say quite loudly, 'I tell you I haven't a notion!' and the drumming on the door stopped. I heard Liam walk back over to us and there was a funny sort of silence, like when everyone in the room is staring at one person.

Liam said, 'I have the tickets', and there was a smile in his voice when he said it that made me smile too. Miss Puddie made a little snort in her nose that didn't sound very friendly and the two of them moved away from the door towards the platform.

I practically ran home, partly because I did not want Daddy to know I had been out, but partly because I was so excited at my adventure.

When Daddy got home I was asleep in the chair by the hearth and everything in the house was spick and span. He touched me gently on the shoulder and I woke up knowing exactly where I was this time. I followed his eyes as they took in the clean table and the swept floor. He turned to me and I saw the drinky look on him.

'You look better,' he said, but his words were too close together. I nodded and looked away into the fire. After a moment I heard him moving towards the stairs, fast steps and then a stop and then some more fast steps until he was gone.

Liam came in not long after. He looked very tired, like when he has been unclogging a drain. He looked at me too, and though he said nothing at first, he had a watery look about him that was very affectionate.

'Ron,' he said at last, but I didn't feel like laughing. I looked right back at him and my look said clearly, 'Well?'

Liam pulled the theatre ticket stubs out of his pocket and ran them between his finger and thumb for a moment with a frown on his face. Then he turned back to me and grinned.

'Very dramatic,' he said, and threw them into the fire.

When I was alone again, I thought that I did not like the way Molly Puddie spoke to Liam that night. It puzzled me that he should have chosen a sweetheart who did not like him. I was just tired, though, and mysteries do not stay mysteries for long if a person really thinks about them. As I settled into my bed I realised what the answer was: she must be as beautiful as a flower.

Four

My darling Alicia's hip against mine guides my progress these days as my eyes once did. I imagine to the casual observer we look rather like any other elderly couple, strolling arm in arm on a chilly autumn morning in Dublin city. Perhaps a curious sort of person might notice a lack of focus in my gaze, but I doubt it. Most observers *are* casual unless it suits them to be otherwise.

In my practice, I long ago discovered that a person's occupation seems to shape their senses. I examined a watchmaker once who complained of a deterioration of his visual acuity so subtle that my instruments barely registered it. The man was stooped double with a severe scoliosis that must have caused him agonising pain, but, hunched over at a perfect angle to ply his trade, he noticed only his minutely altered vision.

When I could see, I accepted the received wisdom that a blind person's other senses sharpen to compensate for the missing one. It's not quite so. What frees the other senses is simply a paring down – a lack of distraction. One simply has more energy to make sense of what one hears or touches, liberated from the beautiful assault of vision.

My blindness was instant and profound. Alighting from the sleeper train at Euston Station, my hands shuffling through the pages of the speech I would give to the British Medical Association, I slipped and fell. Concerned hands manoeuvred me upright: fully conscious, both retinas fully detached.

I have never found the time to mourn my sight. I mourned those lost pages, scattered into the utter blackness of the platform of Euston Station. I had written them in haste, fired with excitement at the audiences I had been granted with the three legendary surgeons I had travelled to the continent of North America to seek. I would never journey so far again.

Weeks later in a nursing home in Shooters Hill, my head immobilised between sandbags, I listened to Alicia's pen scratching across a page, crossing out and scribbling again, trying to make coherent my confused dictation. But I could no more recall the words I had let fall than I could see.

My shoe made a hollow, clunking sound on the loose paving stone near our home.

'Well?' I asked my wife, 'what's the bicycle count?'

Alicia's voice had a smile in it. She thinks I can somehow sense the distance to the house. I haven't let her in on all my little tricks, vain man that I am.

'Not a one,' she said. 'Thank God for student debauchery, they must have all drunk themselves stupid last night.'

My wife has a low opinion of our budding MDs and surgeons and thinks they pester me. If the truth be known, I relish their consultations and I was just a little put out that the railing wasn't groaning with abandoned bicycles.

'O, wait ...' she said. 'There's a car. It's... that's John Geraghty's.'

I must have made a sound.

'Don't you snort at me, Dr Daft-as-a-Coote. He keeps a busy lizzy on the back seat, for some reason; his car's like the Botanic Gardens on wheels, it wouldn't take Sherlock Holmes.'

Sheila had deposited him in my study, and had obviously looked after him reasonably well, for he rattled Alicia's best china as he rose to greet us. I heard a sound that I took to be tea hitting a valuable Persian rug from a great height, and my wife's murmured, 'Ah you're grand, John,' overlaid by John Geraghty's customary 'O' of mortification. The boy, as I recollect, is eighty per cent limbs.

'How have you been doing, sir?' he asked.

I remember a time when he didn't treat me like a typhoid patient. My wife cut across me rudely.

'He's like an infernal bore, is what. He got five pounds off Frank Aveling in a rubber of bridge last night, him and that chancer Brennan – you know, the liver man – and he's been crowing about it since he opened his eyes this morning.'

God increase my wife, she's the only person who can mention my eyes without choking on it. John Geraghty, on the other hand, was swamped with the choice of issues to fret over.

'Bridge? I mean … Of course, that's wonderful … Good for you! I just … How did … O …'

'Braille deck, John,' I said. 'And would you ever sit down and relax for yourself, you're rattling the pattern off my wife's best china.'

Alicia beat a tactful retreat at this point, well aware that John Geraghty is one of those old-fashioned young men who cannot talk fluently in front of a woman, no matter what her age. It is a great mercy that his surname is a common one. I for one would not like to be relying on him to perpetuate it.

I do like the chap, however. For one thing he's a damn fine doctor: his thin, blotchy face, peering over ill-fitting spectacles, was a reliable fixture at my clinics at Sir Patrick Dun's. As I got to know him better, I began to see through his unprepossessing exterior to the keen mind within. It is not difficult for a smart student to learn from the experts, but John's great gift was that he included his patients in that category. I have rarely met a doctor who paid such scrupulous attention to his patients, teasing out from them the precise nature of their suffering. After all, no one has a greater knowledge of an ailment than the person who has it, and even as a student he never made the mistake of trying to shoehorn his patients into a diagnosis for which he had a name.

Make no mistake; this did not always endear him to his professors or indeed his other patients. John Geraghty took case notes from a gouty farmer as if that farmer was an eminent surgeon, and as a result he was one of the slowest doctors in the history of Irish medicine. Indeed, just after he qualified, a fellow student dressed a skeleton and left it in the waiting room of the surgery where he was serving as locum, much to the amusement of his other patients if not to John himself. I am told he has since speeded up somewhat.

I hadn't seen the chap for many months, but this didn't surprise me. It was now five years since my blinding and I was becoming used to a gradual falling off in the attention of those who were not my nearest and dearest. This was quite as it should be. In *Coriolanus*, Shakespeare made the human body a metaphor for the state, but it is more like a metaphor for humanity itself. When the body is wounded, all the energies and healing resources rush to the site and minister to it, and as the wound starts to heal the rest of the body goes back to its usual working. People, too, crowd around an ailing member and then ebb away and return to their previous concerns.

In my profession, perhaps more than most, I had encountered other people's tragedies and I recognised the desire to be close to catastrophe. A curious person yearns to press their vital flesh against the maimed or dead to see how they feel and smell. I had attended funerals of people I scarcely knew and joined with the rest of the congregation in straining my neck to catch a glimpse of the most bereaved to see what would be written on their faces or revealed in their bodies' gait. I also knew the acute embarrassment of meeting, months later, a person whose hand I had held too warmly at a wake, not quite knowing how to reverse the intimacy.

The curve of my acquaintance with John Geraghty had been textbook thus far. We had been esteemed professor and respectful student and then mentor and protégé. After my own personal trauma he had been more present, and I as victim had been grateful. As I regained myself he had faded away, along with all the others. Now he was sitting in my parlour, and I wondered why.

I was answered soon enough.

'I've come about a girl,' he said.

My astonishment must have registered on my face, for he immediately reverted to his old, blustering self and started frantically qualifying his last pronouncement.

'A patient! I mean a patient. I've come about a patient. She's a girl … a she, I mean. I've come about a girl patient. A patient. Not a girl. As such.'

'Yes, John. All right, you've fully established her gender, thanks very much,' I interrupted, unable to bear it any longer. Since the truth had clearly emerged in the opening statement, I welcomed the forthcoming conversation like a barrister whose client has just pleaded, 'Guilty. I mean, *not* guilty!' Our only son, Robert, was well married by now, so I thought I had finished dispensing birds and bees wisdom. However, I rather relished the thought of sharing with my wife the image of John Geraghty in love.

'Please, Professor Coote …' said John in an anguished voice.

'Edward,' I threw in, wearily, for the millionth time in our relatively short acquaintance.

'*Edward!*' he bellowed back at me.

I was quite taken aback at hearing my own name yelled across at me at such a volume. Clearly, the boy was under some stress so I modified my somewhat snide tone and inquired more gently, 'All right. Let's start again, shall we?'

'I'm sorry, Profess … *Edward*,' he said after a couple of quite audible calming breaths. 'It's just that I have … a dilemma.' He started to tell me about the girl.

'Morrie Halpin asked me to examine her – you know Morrie, I think?'

I did indeed – an excellent fellow. I had treated his father some years ago for a virulent cancer of the lungs and although he succumbed in the end, I think it is fair to say that we gifted a year to him through our efforts. Morrie certainly believed so, for he threw himself into a series of inventive schemes to raise funds for my hospital, Sir Pat's.

My most recent memory of him was at a dinner to celebrate the wireless – I never will get used to toasting inanimate objects – in the Royal Dublin Society, where Alicia regaled me with detailed descriptions of his wife Kitty's voluminous gown and her suspicions that it concealed a joyful secret.

The untimely death of Maurice senior, whose beloved Clara had predeceased him many years before, had left Morrie a very wealthy young man. An only child, he was a dabbler by nature and he and his energetic love, Kitty, glided through a bewildering array of charitable schemes and occupations. He joined the army and managed to avoid every major conflict of the present century, and by the time he left he had founded more leisure societies than Trinity College offers during Freshman Week.

Morrie had apparently approached John about his niece. I felt a momentary pang of jealousy. Had I not lost my sight I had no doubt that he would have approached me, but people have little confidence in a blind surgeon.

'I got there early, you see,' he said. 'They live in Shannack, and I thought that I didn't know where that was. But it turns out … I did …' he finished lamely.

It crossed my mind at this point that John really ought to be discouraged from speaking to people; it could foster an unacceptable lack of confidence in the profession as a whole. However, as he continued to unfold his story, his hesitancy abated. It seemed as if he became mesmerised by his own tale. This was not a new phenomenon to me: people act differently when they feel they are not observed.

'I got no reply at the door, so I went around the back to see if there was anyone there. The door was open, of course, you know the way it is in the country.'

I happen to know that Shannack lies not fourteen miles from the capital, but John Geraghty is a city boy – his motor car's bucolic backseat notwithstanding – so I didn't contradict him and merely nodded.

'It's a terrible house, really. A squat little labourer's cottage, neglected, you know? On the outside anyway, more so than the usual. Not just workaday, but really… tired looking, like there was no man around, and there are two of them. The father and a son.'

His voice had changed and I would almost

swear that he was no longer looking at me. He had moved into the confessional.

'It's at the foot of the hills. It's a very wooded place, Shannack, deciduous trees right up to the summit – quite beautiful actually. The trees start right flush up against their backyard, like the house was gouged out of them, if that makes sense. She was standing among the trees.'

There are times in your life when you realise that something quite strange is occurring. For example, little pleases Alicia and I more than dining with friends. On occasion, though, something intangible shifts the dining into an Epicurean idyll – not the food, you understand, but the idyll of the actual philosopher Epicurus: a perfect communion. Sometimes I am aware that I will remember a particular meal until my dying day, such harmony and truth attends it. I knew I would remember John Geraghty's story for a long time. He spoke fitfully, as if he were snatching at the images that crowded his mind.

'She was picking wildflowers. I frightened her. She turned around and ... I was caught unawares. She had a scarf around her head. Around her mouth. All I could see were her eyes. She has the most extraordinary eyes!'

'Yes?' I said. I was thrown by the violent intimacy. I so wanted to hear more that I uttered the question as one would to a child who is struggling to explain their pain.

'Yes! They were ... everything was ... *in them.*'

I am seldom lost for words, but I was now. I tried to remember the correct way to arrange my face to encourage intimacy. Alicia knows me so well that I never have to draw her out, and I had forgotten how to do it. I fear I may have looked constipated. I was aware that some delicate thread was being woven and I was breathless with fear of breaking it. I am an old man, tragedy has made me a selfish one, but I was astounded by the vulnerability of the boy.

'She ...' John stopped. Silence staled between us. When he spoke next I realised that something had been lost.

'She ... she presents with a cleft lip and palate which has never been treated. I mentioned the eyes and all, because ... just to say that I didn't see her mouth until ... later.'

He was back to his bumbling self, the spontaneity of the past moment gone, but what he had just said more than piqued my interest afresh.

'Here's the thing, Profess ... Edward. Her father was completely hostile to the idea of treatment. He didn't seem to want her examined at all and when I mentioned surgery to him he went ... well, *berserk*. I don't think Morrie had really discussed an operation with him. In fact, I wonder what he thought I was there for. I wanted to ask you ...'

'Yes?'

'What to ... what course of action would be appropriate? I think it ... I'm not sure what I should do. For the best. For ... her.'

'What age is the girl?' I asked avidly.

'Fourteen.'

Fourteen. A fourteen-year-old girl with an untreated cleft lip and palate. In this day and age it is rare indeed for a child to reach puberty without some attempt being made to correct such a condition. No, not rare – *unique*; and this child was a niece of Morrie Halpin, one of the most energetic 'fixers' I have ever encountered.

Aside from the obvious psychological implications of living life with a facial disfiguration, the girl would have done well to avoid infections caused by misdirected food and any number of other complications. It is a sad fact of our shallow modern life, of course, that one of those complications was that the girl would be completely unmarriageable.

I had obviously misinterpreted John Geraghty's passionate interest in the girl's case. He must simply have felt enormous empathy with this unfortunate child.

'Has the father actually refused to have her treated?'

'No-o-o, not in so many words, but he refused to bring her to Dublin for a follow-up visit. I'm sure I would never have seen her again if ... I gave him my telephone number, you see. There's a telephone in Shannack post office; I didn't think he'd use it.'

'But he did?'

'The next day. She was sick, he said. He was screaming down the telephone, nearly took the ear off me, wanting to know what I'd done to her. Threatened to slice my ...' He stopped himself, presumably in deference to my august presence. Actually, I'd love to have heard the details.

'Well, he was ... quite *rude*, let's say, but I hadn't done a thing, I only looked at her!' He was getting a bit hysterical.

'Well of course, John, get a grip on yourself, man! I hardly think you go about poisoning your patients.' I said. I couldn't resist adding, 'Not on a first visit anyway, you would hardly know them.'

'Professor Coote!' He said indignantly, and then, when the penny finally dropped, 'O, I see. A joke.'

I had forgotten that he has almost no discernible sense of humour. It used to vex me hugely during lectures, for I have a stock of top-notch anecdotes and he was merely the dourest of a particularly humourless year.

'Proceed,' I said, dispiritedly.

'I raced down in the motor car. Pretty nervous, actually,' he said with a mirthless titter.

'So I would imagine,' I replied, mildly.

'You see, her father said she was raving and fevered. I felt guilty, like it was my fault.'

'O, for the love of God, John! I've told you—' I started, exasperated, but he cut in on me.

'No. I don't mean ...' and he sighed a deep sigh, like a schoolmaster compelled once more to explain a simple sum.

'It started to rain when we were in the yard, we

ran for the house but I slipped and fell in the mud. We both got a fit of the giggles and we just … stayed there … laughing. We were there a long time. Laughing. In the rain.'

There it was again! That love-struck schoolboy phraseology. The man seemed inordinately senti-mental about this girl. I made a mental note to inquire if Alicia had spotted any Penny Dreadfuls or sentimental novels sticking out of his pocket, anything that might explain this rather unsettling mawkishness.

The image of John Geraghty overcome by mirth did not sit well with me either. Since I can no longer take visual clues from people's faces, I am thrown when the content of their speech betrays a change in their character.

'She had to change her clothes, you see, she was so wet,' he continued, sounding a little less dramatic. 'I thought maybe she had caught a chill, that's why I felt responsible … irresponsible, actu-ally,' he added, miserably.

'And had she?' I inquired.

'Had she what?'

'Caught. A. Chill.' I replied, rather more impa-tiently than I intended.

'No,' he said simply.

I hardly needed to enjoin him to continue. So I waited, certain that an insecure man like John Geraghty would not be able to stand the silence between us for long. Only truly confident people can do this, I have found, and almost no Irish person under the age of fifty can manage it. After a couple of breaths that sounded like false starts, he said, 'She was drunk.'

'*Drunk!*' I spluttered out. 'Are you sure?'

'I should know,' he said quietly.

I stifled my surprise and let a moment pass, but this time no elaboration was forthcoming. Whatever John Geraghty's experience of drunkenness was, he clearly did not intend to unbosom himself to me.

It seemed hardly credible that such a diligent student could have been a toper himself, but then, I reflected, young men are quite capable of functioning on quantities of alcohol that would fell an older one. Something told me not to inquire further.

Silence began to fill the space between us, and this time I was unsettled. I found myself sucking air over my teeth and shaking my head: the inarticulate Irish way of commenting without utterance.

'What kind of man lets his child get drunk in the middle of the afternoon?' he said at last, his voice petulant with distress.

'Well, man! He obviously didn't know!' I said. 'Didn't you just tell me he rang you because he thought she was sick?' He made no answer.

I was beginning to feel frustrated by the exchange. It was like talking to a sticky-faced child who clams up when the stolen cake is mentioned.

In my mind's eye John Geraghty's lip was quivering, his finger fiddling with the hem of his short pants. This was supposed to be a consultation!

I stood up suddenly, steadied myself and paced the seven steps to the drinks cabinet: a short journey over the most threadbare piece of carpet in the house. Alicia says she can always tell when I am about to have a drink, as those seven footsteps are no longer muffled.

Although it was far earlier than my habit, I selected a heavy cut crystal tumbler and uncorked a fine whiskey: my favorite for many reasons, not least the unusually rotund shape of the bottle, which made it instantly recognisable to me. I was sick of pouring an inch of liquid into a tumbler and finding it to be wine.

This was the real thing, though. A fine whiskey assaults all the senses I have available. I poured rather more of it down my throat than usual: it actually made my eyes water. As I slammed the glass back down on the cabinet, I realised that I was angry and behaving like a character in a melodrama; stalking across the room and necking a drink like a parody of a man under stress.

I have many faults, but self-delusion is not one of them. I had been unfair in designating John Geraghty the child in our exchange, for there were two.

As soon as the boy mentioned that his patient was an adult with a facial disfigurement, an old excitement stirred in me. I did not want to discuss some ignorant old farmer's drunken daughter or agonise whether it is ethical to sit chortling in the mud if influenza is the likely outcome. Let me be quite frank: I wanted to play God.

I have said that I am a vain man, but that small word scarcely expresses the precise identification I have had with the Deity.

In the hot, dead air of Gallipoli I looked down on the mangled faces of young men who were going to survive. *We* had given life back to them, toiling among the flies and the filth of the medical centre. One youngster, I remember, stared past me as I examined his wounds. His mouth was fixed in a grotesque one-sided grin, the product of a gaping rent in his face that exposed his teeth; he would forever wear a jaunty death's head.

I felt the horror of God: the power to give life, without the power to ensure that that life is joyful. Make no mistake, God must be wracked with sobs for his creatures. He must, or his son's humanity taught him nothing.

Sometimes it is hard not to conclude that there is anything but random caprice directing the affairs of man, but then there are the mysterious ways: we learned so much in the crucible of the Great War. Slowly, painstakingly, we started to learn the ways to put those young men back together. That work did not end after the war, and, to my mind, the field of reconstructive surgery became the single most dynamic area of surgical advance.

The pages that disappeared into the blackness of Euston Station were a gathering together of years of research, my own and others, and a proposal to pool information across the continents on new reconstructive surgical techniques. To put it another way: fixing faces was my 'thing'.

Geraghty, of course, knew this and that was why he had brought this child's story to me. I needed to find a patience I didn't feel to let him continue.

'Drink, John?' I said and instantly regretted it, concerned that I might have just stepped on another conversational mine. His reply, however, reassured me.

'Em, no thanks, Profess … Edward. It's a little early for me.'

His tone was distracted, as if the subject of whether to have a drink was of little importance to him. So, not a toper then.

I set the glass down on the cabinet and paced slowly back to my chair. It was time to take control of this unsettling exchange.

'John,' I said in my most avuncular voice. 'Am I to understand that you have come here to ask my advice?'

'Yes,' he said simply.

'Then do me a great favour and button up for the next while and listen to me.'

There was a pause.

'Mmm,' he ventured.

'Go back to this man and make it impossible for him to *refuse* treatment for his daughter! Confront him with his neglect if necessary, browbeat him if you must, but stamp your authority on the situation. *Then* we can start to have fun!'

'I really don't think her father—' began Geraghty weakly, but I cut across him, pounding on the arm of the chair for emphasis.

'For God's sake, you are a doctor, man! What is he but a poor labourer?'

Then I remembered his strange attachment to the girl, so I added, 'We will make that disfigured child a footnote to history. I haven't seen a single case of an adult with a cleft lip and palate since before the Great War; you have no *idea* what we could achieve.'

There was a rather blank silence, which I hardly thought appropriate for such stirring words, so I resorted to barking at him.

'O, get down there and be a man! If you do not you have failed her.'

It is strange how silences have different flavours. It seemed to me that this time I could hear my words sinking into him, turning in his mind. Then I heard him stand, the crack of a knee straightening.

'Thank you, Professor,' he said, and walked out of the room. I didn't bother to correct him.

Some moments later Alicia came in, her comfortable smell warming the room. 'What under heaven did you *say* to that boy?' she said from the door. 'He looked like Parsifal.'

I smiled to myself, overlaying John Geraghty's lanky form onto the golden knight in my wife's favorite painting.

'Well, well, my clever Alicia, that is because I have sent him on a quest.'

Alicia did not answer straight away, but I could sense her disquiet. She rounded my chair and came to stand in front of me. I knew she was regarding me; even blind I could see her tilting her head and setting her jaw as she tried to read my thoughts.

'O, Edward,' she said at length, and her voice had tears in it. 'I have liked you so much more these last five years.'

I reached out for her hand, disturbed by the sound of her. She did not come to meet it, and I groped the air before I could clasp her.

'He is consulting me about a patient!' I said, in my most reassuring voice. 'A young woman with a harelip we are going to fix, that is all. We are going to make a disfigured little girl into a pretty young lady.'

'I see,' said Alicia, her tone betraying nothing. 'Then, husband, may I ask you a question?'

'Of course,' I replied, warily.

She didn't speak immediately, but let her hand lie limp in mine. Then she said quietly, 'What is her name?'

I never said about the mystery bird. I used to think it was a she, but then Cass told me that birds sing to get a wife to come to them. It was Mammy who called it the mystery bird, or at least I think it was. Sometimes I remember things about Mammy, but the annoying thing is I don't know if they are real memories or just made up.

In my head I see her standing in the yard looking up at the trees with a cloth in her hands as if she had just come out from wiping the plates. She has a wondering look on her face, but then she also has a light all around her and that can't be right. I wish there was something particular that would make me know it was real, like if maybe she had a pair of red shoes on her and then somebody you hadn't seen for donkeys' years might chance to say, 'I remember those red shoes your Mammy used to wear,' and then I would know. The thing about birds is that you don't know if they are ordinary or dreams.

In the spring I hear all kinds of sounds from the birds in the trees outside my window. I love those sounds, though I don't know which birds they belong to unless I can see them. But the mystery bird is louder than any of them and he sings like he is trying to stand out from the crowd, but you can't see him no matter how hard you try. Maybe he thinks he doesn't look very nice.

Funnily enough, the birds Daddy catches don't sing even though he calls them songbirds. The only sounds they make are flapping sounds and hitting noises when they go against the sides of the cage. I suppose you don't sing when you're frightened, I know I don't.

The mystery bird sings everything twice. He sounds happy and bold, and that sound makes me want to get up. Sometimes a person doesn't feel like getting out of bed and doing all the things that need doing, but the mystery bird makes you want to draw your hands through the sheet and feel the air.

I heard him this morning. The pain and the hotness were so distracting that I almost missed him, but then the song seeped into my mind and made me forget about my belly for a moment.

I raised myself up on my elbows and I listened. He made a little burst of loud, bright song and then stopped short, as if he had said exactly the right thing. Then he sang it again, faster than a person could play on a penny whistle, and then he stopped again.

My ears strained to listen to the crisp, clear silence. It seemed like his voice had made a spell on the air, but I must have woken up just at the end of his performance, for in a moment the air clouded over and became just ordinary again; he must have flown away.

The mystery bird had distracted me, but now the pain came back, stronger than before. Once, when Liam made a great rent in his finger with the scissors, Daddy had to put salty water on the cut and he told me to 'distract' him. I didn't know the word, but somehow I knew what he wanted me to do. We were both little and a little child's thought came to me. I ran to the sink and I got the big saucepan and I put it on my head and ran around not able to see. Then I felt a big crash and I fell over. Liam and I were both wailing now, but Daddy howled with laughter till the tears came in his eyes.

The ache in my belly was growing stronger and the thing that made the pain worse was that I didn't know what it was. I was fearful and I rocked back and forward to see if I could make the aching turn into something else. My body felt restless, as if I needed to do something but I couldn't think what.

All of a sudden I felt a spurt of something coming out of me. I stopped rocking and just sat there. There was wetness around the hinge of me and my stomach hurt with a big, dull pain.

I wanted to look at the wetness and I leaned down over myself to do it, but my arms wrapped around myself instead and I hugged the pain and stared ahead.

When you want to be sick, the badness pulls up inside you and heads for your throat. This sickness was different: it was like the badness was down so deep that it was underneath the way up. All of a sudden I wanted to turn around and press my belly into the bed, so I did in a rush. The sickness just shifted around to my back.

With my face in the pillows, I could feel sweat trickling over the backs of my ears. It was hard to breathe, so I sat up again. The covers were bunched around me and my night things had rucked up underneath. I pulled them up further and I looked between my legs. When you cut your finger the blood is fresh and clear like pouring water. What I saw between me was old blood, thick bits of jelly blood, like jam coming from boiling sugar. I was bleeding blood that looked like you could eat it. I couldn't think where I was bleeding from. I felt a hot worry coming up from the place where the blood was, and the aching seemed like a pump inside me.

I stared at the blood as it soaked through the sheet and I watched the colour get weaker as it spread outwards, making a little halo of stain around itself. My face looking down felt heavy, like the blood inside my skin was all at the front. All my blood was throbbing in a dull, low rhythm.

I pushed my finger across the sheet and it jerked along the cotton until it came to the sticky, cold stain. I followed it upwards and I let my finger slide back to where the wetness came out. It was soft there. I stayed for a long time in a daze, feeling the warm place and wondering why the pain there was not sharp like cuts usually are.

I tried to imagine what it would be like if Cass could see me. I tried to picture her in front of me to see could I work out would she be relaxed and light-hearted, or upset; like when she said she was a careless old bitch. But even though I felt very serious about it all, I couldn't help thinking that if she really was in front of me looking at me, she would be squeezed in flat between the bed and the wall, with her curly hair getting tangled up in the broken looking glass.

One thing was, she would know what the mystery bird was. When a bird is around, Cass always has a bird name for it. I only ever see a black flash going out of view, but she sees things slowed down.

Once, when we were walking by the river, she asked me what a bird was, and I said I didn't know, I had only seen them moving, so to speak. Then

Cass asked me what colour it was, and she said it like it was an easy clue that would help me. I said that it was black and she laughed.

'We're graced with a kingfisher that would take the eyes out of a duchess hungry for jewels, and the child sees a crow!'

I felt very stupid, and I wished that the bird would come back, for I wanted to see the jewels now that I knew they were there. The curious thing was that when I thought about the flash again, I thought I could remember blue and tawny orange. I just said black because I had to give an answer and I hadn't any thinking over to remember what I had seen.

I thought it would be good if I gave some time to thinking about the blood between my legs, so that I could see if I knew what it was if I thought more slowly. I thought for a while and all that I could come up with was that I wanted someone to talk to.

Cass. I wanted to talk to Cass.

I felt like her. I am a little person. My body is a small thing and I always feel the material in my skirts bunched up and empty; but right now I felt full. It seemed as if there was some liquid under my skin that ballooned me out and made me solid like Cass.

Then a thought struck me. Perhaps the thing that was filling me out and making me bleed was Cass's green wine. I wondered if she always felt like this: bleeding and full. Maybe all her clothes were to let the blood have a place to seep into. Cass might be sick with wine and now I might be too.

I looked at my hands. They were pinky with blood and trembling. I breathed in deeply to try to get back to myself, and I decided there and then to stop all the thinking about things and get on with it. I felt queer, that is for certain, but that was no reason for a person to let their head run away with them.

I packed the middle of the sheet against where the blood was. I didn't know quite how I could get about like that, so I took the matter into my own hands and decided to sacrifice the sheet entirely. I stretched over to the top corner of the bed and I pulled at the edge of it to loosen it from under the mattress.

I never before thought that I would have a reason to give out to myself for being too good a bed-maker, but I did now. I nearly ruptured myself trying to get that blessed sheet free. I listened for a moment to the quiet in the house before I did the next thing: one big snoring, Liam was asleep. Of course, it being Sunday, Daddy would be out since first light trapping the songbirds to sell behind the Protestant cathedral in Dublin city. So that was all right.

Slowly, so as not to make a big noise, I ripped a narrow band like a bandage from the edge of the sheet. The top part was the hardest, where it was sewn, but I opened the stitching with my teeth and I did the same at the end. I made strip after strip, and when the cloth on one side of me was all rags, I did the same on the other side. Then I tore the cloth from in front of me and behind and I was free.

Standing up made me feel sick, and I had to walk like a duck to keep the rags in tight against me. I threw open the casement to feel the cold. The pain in my belly didn't go away, but the air woke up my head. I was all action now. I knew what the best thing to do would be, so I set about doing it.

I packed clean rags against me, and let the bloody ones fall to the floor. I dressed quickly, for the morning air was cold on my hot skin, and I used my undergarments to hold the clean cloths in place.

I picked up the basin and I carried it carefully to the window. It was funny to see the water moving flat in the bowl, like it didn't care what way the bowl was tilted; it was going to stay as it was.

The yard below looked mean. From the window, you couldn't see any of the nice things about the house, like how clean the step is or how there are two blue bowls in the kitchen window. All you could see was the low wall around the pigs, and the pigs mooching around each other heavily. Our yard was horrible when you looked at it and then at the trees beside it. It showed the trees up, really.

I gave one big throw with the basin and I watched the water splat down on the ground. It sounded like someone being slapped. In the quiet after that sound I listened again for snoring. It was there, though it was hard to tell it from the grunting in the sty.

When I dried out the basin with more of the clean sheet I placed it on the window ledge. I picked up the bloody cloths from the floor, and my stomach felt weighty as I bent over. I put them in the middle of the white bowl and I had a curious fancy that they were bits of some broken up flowers set in the middle of a feast day table.

I brought over the lamp matches and I struck one, covering it from the outside air with my hand. The little flame caught the thready edge of the cloths, and it tried hard to light up, fighting with the breeze. I watched the white middle of the fire get lost in orange, and smoke started to fill the bowl and blow into my eyes, making tears come. It surprised me how quickly the fire took the cloths, and even when it fizzed over the blood it didn't stop, but took that too.

When it was finished, and the last bright orange thread turned to black, I tossed the ash out of the window. The inside of the bowl was singed brown, but the thought came to me, 'What of that?'

I went down into the silent house so quickly that I must have reached the kitchen at the same time as the ash settled on the earth of the yard.

I was hot and I started to imagine things that were not there. I will say the things I saw in my mind's eye, even though I know they were not real because they happened so quickly and were so strange.

I saw a child sitting newly upright on the floor, looking at the window. She was perfect. Even though her back was to me, I knew her mouth was parted right across the middle, where a mouth should part. She let the rosebud parts pucker and lift to the cold sky. She was kissing the light.

Under the picture of her there was no distress, no mammy touching her breasts and sobbing, no daddy draining a bottle and staggering up to an empty bed: only stillness.

In my daydream I felt things sliding off my back and leaving me weightless. People entered the room bearing flowers. Flat, plate-shaped flowers and weird, long ones that reared up out of turned back petals. Things like orchids.

I said things. I said words out of my bright mouth. I couldn't quite understand the things I said, but all the people who listened were smiling and wet-eyed hearing them. Everything that a mouth could say came out like spit honey, sweetening the places it landed.

And then I started to spit mud. I said dirt things. I said all the things that are inconvenient. Closet things came rushing out of my pretty mouth and they shot into the air and drove away the crowd.

I was standing at the stairs but I could see the space in the room where the light from the window made a square for my mouth self to sit. The words were infecting and changing the air. I could see pus curdling in the air like buttermilk. It fell to the swept floor in pearly drops, and rolled away from me as if I was sitting on a high hill.

I smelled him before I saw him and it pulled me back to reality. He was standing in the front doorway.

He looked like a frog. I was so distracted by the thoughts in my head that the first thing he said sounded to my ears like 'ribbit'.

I knew I had heard wrong and that he couldn't really be talking like a frog so I tried to find a way of knowing what he had said.

I moved the skin between my eyes as much as to say, 'What?'

He instantly understood for he replied, 'Is your father ... ?' He let his face go wavy instead of saying the last word. The space between us felt thick and I said nothing.

I could see his face reddening, like blood was creeping up it. Then he said this: 'Veronica.' Real soft, and he took a step towards me, holding his hand out in front of him.

I ran out of the house until I reached the trees. It was cool there and I thought I might think better. I looked over to the door, but he did not come out; after all, he was looking for Daddy. It puzzled me that I had not put my hand to my mouth when he looked at me, but I suppose I was not quite myself when he came in.

Much more curious was the fact that he was standing in the kitchen at all. He surely could not know about the bleeding, for nobody knew about that except me. My belly was still heavy and sore, so I slid down to sit on the crunchy leaves and leaned my back against a tree.

It was nicer to be out in the air, and the cold was dulling the heat under my skin. It made my mind a little calmer and I thought it through.

He must be very brave to come back here when Daddy had been so horrible to him. That seemed odd to me, for brave people don't usually do so many cringey things with their head. Even so, he must have had good reason for coming back, for doctors are busy men.

I could only think of two reasons, and one of them was good and one of them was bad.

Maybe, being a doctor, he had guessed about the wine and the imaginings and he knew I was going mad. That was the bad thing.

But maybe he was here to make Daddy get my mouth fixed.

Suddenly, from high up in the woods, I heard the sound of the cages clinking off each other and the fainter sounds of the panicking birds inside them. Daddy was coming.

As he came nearer I began to fear that Dr Geraghty would go before he got to the house, so I scrambled to my feet and I ran towards the house. I stopped my running by grabbing the sides of the door and I hung there, panting, looking at the spot where he had been, but he was gone.

I rushed through the kitchen to the front door, hitting off the table in my haste and making some thing or other fall with a smash. A black, shiny motor car stood outside our house with Dr Geraghty's legs sticking out of the side of it. It was so close to the door that I must have been deaf not to hear it when he arrived. There seemed to be a big plant growing inside the car and for a moment I thought it was swallowing him.

When he straightened up again he was holding a metal bar with a handle. He saw me, but this time he stayed where he was. I was staring at the bar.

'Just going to crank her up!' he said. I couldn't think who he was talking about, but then I realised he meant the motor car.

I didn't say anything because I had no idea what cranking up was. So I just stayed where I was and my hand came up to my mouth. I must have been feeling more myself.

His face got sad then like he wished I hadn't put my hand there.

'I'm making a bit of a habit of scaring you,' he said. 'I did knock, Veronica, but you were miles away.'

I heard all the words, and I knew what they all meant, but my own name seemed loudest of all, like when you shout into a well.

'*Veronica!*'

Daddy's voice came from the kitchen, followed very fast by Daddy. It was funny, for he hung from the front door by his arms exactly as I had just hung from the back door. He was panting too.

'Jesus! I thought you were ...' he said, but he stopped, seeing Dr Geraghty. Strangely enough, although I felt very serious about it all, I had a lighthearted thought: 'Uh oh. Now there'll be trouble!'

Daddy was looking very serious too. He stopped panting and it seemed like all the air was building up inside him like steam in a kettle.

Nobody said anything for a minute. I had a feeling like when you read an adventure book and the hero is being chased by savages, or fighting a fire-breathing dragon: I was dying to know what would happen next.

'Go around to the yard, Veronica,' said Daddy.

A sound came out of me. I couldn't help it for I was so disappointed I felt like crying.

'Now!' he said in a loud voice, so I had to go.

I thought of staying in the kitchen where I might be able to hear, but I heard them coming in behind me and Dr Geraghty was talking, so I hurried out the back door and I closed it over quietly, but I left a bit of it open. The cages were piled on either side of the door, and the birds were flapping and hitting off the bars. I wished they would not make so much noise so I could hear what was going on inside.

There was talking. I could make out none of the words, but I knew it was Dr Geraghty speaking. He would say some words and then stop, then he would start again. It sounded like he was nervous and the gaps were where he was waiting for Daddy to say something. Then I heard Daddy say something short, and it sounded like a dangerous something, low and growly. Dr Geraghty mustn't have read the signs, or he was braver than I thought, for he immediately started talking back and louder this time.

I swear I didn't touch the door, but slowly it swung a little more open; I think the breeze must have caught it. I could hear the words they spoke.

' ... and Mr Halpin is very concerned indeed, and so am I,' said the doctor.

'*Fuck him!*' shouted Daddy. '*And fuck you!*'

I reached my hand out without thinking and tried to shut the door over. The door met the frame and stopped there for a moment and I didn't have to hear the dreadful scene. Then, just as it had done before, it started to swing towards me very slowly. I think the door is a little warped.

' ... has already put the money in place for her medical care, you have no right to deny her this opportunity when—'

'No right!' Daddy cut in on him. 'You come here to my home, you lanky fuck, with your little bag of savagery and you lay your hands on her for a ...'

I managed to close the door over and I wedged it as tight as I could without making a noise. Then I crossed the yard and stood at the little fence with my fingers pressing onto the soft part of my ears. All the noises were muffled and blended into one, flapping and shouting and oinking. I wished I could whistle or hum, but my mouth cannot do those things, so I tried to have loud thoughts instead.

I thought loudly about the rowan tree in front of me. I thought about its shiny grey bark and the bright red berries that Daddy uses to catch the winter thrushes. I thought about Mammy winding its dark leaves around the churn to protect it from the witches, singing her songs. I thought about the rowan jelly she made when Morrie and Kitty came one Samhain feast because we had a duck to eat. And I thought about its other name, the one Cass uses: mountain ash.

'Veronica.'

Daddy's voice came through my fingers. I turned around to face him and I could see that he was tired. He looked at me with a stare that made me afraid, but then I thought about another thing: Morrie had the money ready for getting me fixed.

'Come inside,' he said.

I felt a strange trickle under my skirts and I looked down. Just as quickly I looked back up again in case I might draw his eyes down too. The blood had come through the rags and it was there on the earth between my feet. I stared back at him.

'In,' he said, but I could not move.

Then a strange thing happened. Daddy made a movement that told me he had given up, and he walked back into the house, sweeping up the cages as he went. I stood listening to him clattering and stamping through the house until I heard the front door slamming. I had disobeyed him and I didn't feel small at all.

I knew then what I must do. I must gather my things into a bundle and I must do it quietly for fear of waking Liam. I must take a pen and paper and write down: Morrie and Kitty Halpin, 23 Fitzwilliam Square, Dublin. I must open the drawer in the kitchen table and take out the beautiful lady banknotes and I must go back to the railway station and get on the train.

So that is what I did.

Six

'Fothergills has no daquoises,' Sheila said baldly.

I let my wife deal with the consequences of her pronouncement and indulged myself in a pedantic dissection of her grammar. I rarely interfere in domestic matters.

Alicia, however, availed of another opportunity to needle me.

'It seems even the patisseries are conspiring against your little cabal,' she said. 'Sheila, it'll be at least an hour and a half before we serve lunch, even if they're on time, which I doubt, so scoot down to

Findlaters and get a brack. They can all choke on that.'

And she strode out of the room. My wife is a single-minded person, and when she is on the war path the sensible man stays perfectly still and pretends to be invisible. I see myself as Antigonus to her Paulina:

'Lo you now! You hear?

When she will take the rein, I let her run.'

I fully expect to exit this life pursued by a bear.

Nonetheless, even by her own standards, her opposition to our project seemed excessive. I mean no disrespect when I say that in many ways my blindness has suited my wife. It fostered a closeness between us that we didn't have when my profession claimed so much of my attention; besides, she has always hated what I do.

In Alicia's mind a surgeon is a creature composed of ego and little more. If I returned home late at night after a punishing round of surgery and lectures, she would offer no sympathy. 'God! Healing the great multitudes puts you in a fierce mood!' she liked to say.

And when colleagues took drinks with us she would often interrupt an intriguing discourse on surgical technique with some ludicrous question. 'Has a patient ever punched you?' is one that stands out in my memory.

I always forgave her, though, for the idea of being married to a simpering little *wifey* held no appeal for me.

Her obsession with this case had a different flavour to it. To be candid, it irritated me that she claimed to be concerned for the girl when I suspected her real fear was quite different. If the profession regained its confidence in me, my dependence upon her might dwindle. She was right to fear it, for the idea excited me.

Even when I made it my business to learn the child's name – Veronica Broderick if it matters – she trumped me.

'And her father? The man whose child you have appropriated? What is *his* name?'

She really is infuriating. At my age I'm doing well to remember my own name; it's all right for her, she can make notes.

I decided that the sun was well over the yardarm; actually I decided that the sun was probably not over the yardarm, but since I cannot see I can hardly be blamed.

I'm not proud to say that I tiptoed over to the drinks cabinet, not wishing to hand more ammunition over to my wife. She is not really a drinker.

I settled back into my chair and let the malty fumes relax me. There is nothing like a fine whiskey to settle a man's mind after a domestic irritation. I have even prescribed it.

In the months since John Geraghty's visit I had been busy. Busier, I should say. My days have always been full even in the last five years. I am a stranger to boredom. Still, it had been a long time since anything had engaged me as completely as this.

Since I lost my sight, only the students made me feel fully useful. I never sought them out, but word of mouth made it known that an oracle resided on Raglan Road, just waiting to be consulted. The visits of my friends and colleagues, on the other hand, seemed to smack of charity. The consultations of the last two months were quite different. Nobody was making himself feel good by visiting Poor Old Coote.

I was now in a position to initiate a single stage operation to correct the child's cleft lip and repair the soft and hard palate. And I had found the optimum surgeon to perform it.

Geraghty had spectacularly failed to persuade the girl's father of anything other than Geraghty's idiocy. I must have been in a dream world when I sent him on that particular errand.

Nevertheless, his visit had an unexpected consequence. The girl took matters into her own hands, forsook her father and presented herself at her aunt and uncle's.

She was quite a sight by all accounts. Effectively mute, she had been unable to ask directions and ended up hopelessly lost in Black Pits. *Not* a safe place for a young woman to find herself, her disfigurement notwithstanding. But luck was on her side, and she arrived in Fitzwilliam Square in state: passenger on a rag and bone cart. She had stumbled upon one of the few literate rag and bone merchants in the city and had shown the address to him. Fortunately for her the man was an upright citizen and delivered her to her relations, albeit slightly mucky and very distressed.

She was now safely ensconced in the Halpin household. It is curious how quickly a person can command affection: Morrie and Kitty became devoted to her almost immediately, although they had scarcely known her beforehand. Morrie claimed that each day now started with a battle of wills between Kitty and Mrs Scallon, her cook, over who would 'get' Veronica.

Actually, he really tells that story most amusingly, culminating in a siege of Troy sequence in which Kitty infiltrates her own kitchen quarters disguised as a Chrysler 77 and carries off 'Helen of Shannack'. Morrie-esque historical inaccuracies abound, needless to say, even in pastiche, but are more than compensated by his motion-picture captions: 'QUICK-THINKING GREEK MOTORIST GETS HEL-ONICA OUT OF A SCRAPE!'

Even I, who had not met her, was moved by her story, and glad that her tribulations were coming to an end. She seemed to be blossoming there.

I was reminded of the words of the great American reconstructive surgeon Leonard Keppel-Stein: 'Sonatas unwritten, poetry unimagined, dreams unrealised and love unbestowed. All lost to the world through the shame of the disfigured. A man needs to glory in himself to bring beauty into being.' Although he wrote those words in the last century, they were just as valid today in 1929.

I caught myself: 1930. Christmas had come and gone, and as usual I was finding it difficult to remember that we had passed into a new year, a new decade in this case. 1930 seemed like a preposterous age for the calendar to have attained. When I was a boy I fully expected to be snug in my tomb by now, or at least so dribbling and senile that it would amount to the same thing. Children are monstrously selfish in their views.

I had considered asking the girl herself to join our little party, for I was immensely curious about her. Still, since I cannot see and she cannot speak it might well have been a futile exercise. And more importantly, we needed to discuss details of the procedure, a task that would be easier without having to pander to her sensibilities. I should not like to frighten the child.

I drained my glass, rather too quickly, and made myself cough. Alicia shot through the door, making the knob hit the wall like a gunshot. I plunged the empty glass down the side of the chair and swizzled it under the cushion: a still humming catapult tucked into the back pocket of a pair of short trousers.

'Sober up, Deity. Your subjects approach,' she said meanly.

I rose to my feet, *perfectly* sober, took her arm rather resentfully, and we walked through to the hall.

Five years ago I used to rail against modernity along with my peers. We were confirmed old fuss-budgets. We complained of the cacophony that the new century had brought in its wake: clanging doorbells, jangling telephones, crackling wirelesses and motor cars chugging up and down the quiet streets, drowning out the hooves.

Now I had changed my tune: I revelled in the noises of the twentieth century. Everything made a racket. If I had been blind from birth I would have spent forty years without hearing jazz in my own parlour or my grandchildren babbling down the telephone receiver in their house in Connecticut: communication with the functionally absent.

The functionally absent Halpins zoomed into our sphere, announcing themselves by the judder-ing cessation of an engine's roar. Alicia opened the door. I felt the cold air on my face and heard the sounds of arrival.

Morrie whooped enthusiastically, banging the side of his motor car and shouting excitedly. 'What do you think of the Edson?'

To my knowledge, he has had five motor cars to date, as he is congenitally incapable of resisting any gadget, no matter how large. I don't know how he expected me to assess the new vehicle, but things like blindness are just finicky details to Morrie Halpin.

'What on *earth* do you do with the old ones?' I inquired as he bounded up the steps to grasp my hand.

'O, you know ...' he said in his merry, vague way, 'sell them and things.'

The unmistakable dark vanilla scent of Kitty drew suddenly near me, and she spoke to me in a mock whisper.

'Three generations of kittens have lived and died in the Bentley. Don't you believe him.' And she kissed me on the cheek in an intimate way that only she could carry off without offence.

Next she turned her attention to Alicia, squealing her appreciation of my wife's invisible attire. Morrie was banging his fists on the wall and saying, 'You should knock that through, Edward! You really should, big halls are absolutely the thing!'

'Don't listen to him,' threw in Kitty, without interrupting her conversation with Alicia. I will never know how women do that.

Only Alicia's gentle 'John' alerted me to his presence, although as soon as he passed me I got the sour, unwashed reek of him. God, that man needs a wife.

We moved into the parlour, as my dearest still styles it. I can never tell if my mind perceives the change of light on my skin, or if my memory recalls the broad sweep of bright window that illuminates our 'good' room.

A colleague in private practice once boasted that he never charged a patient who had no room to put aside. For him it was the ultimate symbol of poverty. I admired him, though I thought him a sentimental fool who would starve if he ever came to work at Sir Patrick Dun's.

Alicia betrayed nothing of her earlier hostility, much to my relief, and was charming hostess incarnate. She bestowed little compliments on the Halpins, which served the additional purpose of creating a thumbnail sketch of the scene for me.

'Kitty! That dress is too lovely, you should always wear that emerald colour, it makes your eyes glow fire! So unusual, though, dear, for you to wear a *high* waist, with all those ruffles at the middle ...' Very little gets past Alicia, she really is a wily old bird.

'Morrie, if I didn't know you better I would think you were examining our house for dust rings: I have never known a man like you for picking up every blessed thing in a house and trying to pull it apart!'

To John Geraghty she said in a quieter voice, 'Do sit down dear, we don't stand on ceremony here.'

I bided my time, allowing our exhuberant guests to wear themselves out a bit. Morrie brayed over to me excitedly about 'minstrel's galleries' and how I really should have one put in. His voice was directed to the ceiling, which I presume he was staking out with a view to persuading me to knock that through too.

'Honestly, Edward, they really act as a *lung* in the house.' I satisfied myself with noncommital responses and wondered what his own house must look like by now. Not a support wall standing, I should imagine.

Kitty ribbed her husband with the passionate air of a devoted wife. 'Morrie! Stop pestering Edward! Come over here and kiss me instead.' Morrie naturally didn't need a second invitation. She really does make me laugh.

'O, Kitty!' said my wife persistently. 'You are positively *blooming!*'

Kitty let a brimming silence impregnate the air, but I could almost see her saucy smile. I'm not at all convinced she didn't actually purr.

Footsteps and delicious smells announced the arrival of the soup. Sheila and Miles (our occasional) stepped gravely about the table dispensing stilton-smelling liquid into the bowls to appreciative 'mmm's.

Still I kept my own council.

After the rather excellent soup, congratulations were offered by all to Alicia for her excellent 'find' in Mr Conaty, our new cook.

'Not Irish, surely!' said Kitty. 'Alicia Coote, you are a *prospector!*'

I made my first overture.

'And how is our own Coppelia?'

There was a silence which I strained to understand. It was broken by Kitty and I was startled to hear tears in her voice.

'She is ... she *seasons* the house,' she said, charmingly.

'Yes,' said Morrie. 'She's really smashing. No trouble at all, except she makes Kit spend all my money.'

I, for one, was none the wiser.

'Keeps buying things to bribe her away from Troy,' he explained.

'I wonder why she feels more comfortable in the servants' quarters?' said Alicia pointedly. I could see exactly where she was heading with that, so I enquired further of Kitty. 'She is happy there, then?'

Kitty suddenly let out a passionate 'O!' and started to sob in a very becoming way.

I struggled to understand; I am not very conversant with feminine tendresses, Alicia not being given to them.

'Not happy?' I said lamely.

'She is the very heart of the house,' Kitty burst out ferverently. 'She gives *meaning* to it. It's like the house was *waiting* for her to come.'

Bizarrely, I heard John Geraghty, of all people, muttering agreement. I was now convinced of something I had suspected for years: Kitty Halpin would have been a *terrific* actress. She really could have rivalled Eleanora Duse for passionate hystrionics.

It was all most satisfactory. I sucked on my claret and imagined the gay assembly, holding up their many-faceted glasses in the light. Well, except for Alicia, who would be sipping from a tumbler of water; she always avoids liquor when she has an axe to grind.

Never mind, it was time to press on.

'I have some news that might interest you,' I said importantly. Silk and stiff collars turned towards me with a swish.

'Tell me something,' interrupted Alicia. The silk and stiff collars whipped around to her. 'Does she miss her home?'

'No!' said Kitty. 'She most certainly does not.'

There was an edge to her voice that I had not heard before, almost predatory. 'In fact, she has never mentioned it,' she concluded emphatically.

No one spoke for a moment, and then Morrie spoke timidly.

'Except ...'

'*Yes*?' pounced Alicia, predictably.

'Except that ... well, she doesn't speak at all.' He was trying to be gentle, not wishing to contradict Kitty, and I rather expected her to challenge him, but to my surprise she remained silent.

'Then how can you be sure that she doesn't miss her home?' persisted my wife.

'We ...' Morrie stopped, and a blind man could tell that he was looking to his wife for permission to continue, that is to say I could tell that.

'Well ... we don't,' he said simply.

At this point I heard a noise of frustration coming from John Geraghty, a vocalisation quickly stifled. Unbelievably, my wife overrode his correct self-censorship.

'Yes, John? You feel differently?'

Geraghty took up the invitation with unseemly eagerness.

'She *can't* miss that hovel! For one thing she is radiant in the Halpins' home. Really, she's blossoming.'

'Exactly!' said Kitty. She really has the most beautiful speaking voice: musical and breathy. 'You should have seen her when the nun came from the laundry to collect the things!' she continued, her voice warming with affection. 'She had spent the morning helping Dolas to sort everything into sacks – she's a wonderful help, you understand – and when Sister Michael came with the magdalenes to take them away, Veronica got terribly distressed. She thought Dolas was giving away all our things! She actually started to cry!' Kitty laughed her glorious laugh, but there was a tinge of wistful sadness in it.

'When Dolas explained that the laundry would come back to us safe and *clean*, she looked like someone had told her that there were eight days in a week!'

'She was treated no better than a magdalene herself in that house,' said Geraghty, unwisely. I found myself wincing involuntarily; I could have told him that you do not make inexact comparisons when my wife is around, *nor* do you criticise nuns.

Alicia, of course, pounced.

'O, I think not, John,' she said in that dangerous, quiet tone of hers that is always an opening salvo. 'You see, she is not a sinner; and furthermore she *grew* there. She was not ripped from a familiar home.' Then to my horror she added, 'Not then.'

A most uncomfortable silence followed. Alicia had, in my opinion, quite contravened the duties of a hostess, for she had made her guests ill at ease and had stopped the flow of conversation. It is her least amiable quality. I would have to salvage the situation, but thankfully I was interrupted by the arrival of lunch.

The natural bustle of clearing and serving bridged the gap, and gave us time to regroup. Glasses were recharged, this time with a crisp sancerre, and a slightly hysterical 'Aah!' greeted the arrival of the lobster.

As our guests admired the crustaceans with something akin to desperation, I retreated into myself and savoured the rich smell of the sea, admixed with scent of lemon butter and fennel. I can eat most dishes and still retain my train of thought, albeit made more pleasurable by the sensations occurring in my mouth, but lobster fills my mind with an image so vivid it is like being smothered by a flag.

Bright red shell, gleaming with trickling butter and touched by delicate fronds of feathery green dill. Until my plate was filled and I had speared the coy, white flesh beneath the shell, I could not regain myself.

It was perfection. I surrendered to the pleasures of the table, and let the murmur of our guests' inconsequential chatter recede from my consciousness. Ignoring completely the array of vegetables on the side of my plate, I let only the sweet crustacean meat enter my mouth, swabbed in lemony butter.

Mr Conaty was indeed a wonderful find. Woman's sphere be damned! The man had elevated the humble craft of cookery to an art form, no matter that he hails from Stranorlar! I am, however, a wise enough male to keep that particular view to myself, particularly in the company of such opinionated females.

When the plates were cleared, Sheila muttered something about dessert, hissing the word '*brack*' in that horrible Dublin accent of hers. I deeply regretted having expressed a preference for a Fothergill's cake, and wished I had left it to Mr Conaty to create one of his foaming marvels.

'I think we'll let the lobster settle for a bit,' I said authoritatively. 'You can bring the brandy and port.'

'And tea, Sheila,' said Alicia.

'Yes, tea,' I concurred, quite sure that she would be the only taker.

I drained my glass and listened to the expectant silence that had settled on the company: they were waiting for me to speak.

'It may interest you to know—' I began, but infuriatingly Alicia interrupted me *again.*

'What does her father say of—'

'*Alicia!*' I cut across her, a little more forcefully than I intended.

Nobody spoke, and I was a little embarrassed by my outburst. Nevertheless, it was time to take control of the meeting, before Alicia's interference overshadowed the exciting developments I had yet, still, to impart.

'I have arranged for Reggie Sweetman to perform a single stage surgery on Veronica,' I said simply.

I waited for my pronouncement to have its effect. It was more gratifying than I could have hoped.

'O, God! O, God! *O, God!*' Kitty's voice was tight and thick with tears.

'Sweetman will! Only you, Edward!' Morrie said, thumping the table and laughing with delight. 'Only you!'

'Sweetman's that beaky man with the face, isn't he?' said Kitty to her husband. 'He's good, isn't he? Isn't he good, Morrie?' They were talking over one another now like excited children.

'Super, absolutely top-drawer. *Just one operation!*'

'That is the hope,' I said calmly. 'We obviously can't be certain until Reggie has a look at her himself, but John here has furnished him with fantastically detailed case notes and he is cautiously optimistic.'

'So this has never been done before?' Morrie said breathlessly, making me splutter with laughter.

'Good God, man! We're not reinventing the wheel! None of the techniques are new, we're just putting them together in a novel way. There's always the chance that we'll have to operate a second time anyway, but, as my mother used to say,

"If you only do what's been done before, you won't do much!"'

The Halpins were obviously overexcited, for this rather feeble aphorism provoked howls of laughter. Morrie actually slapped the table, and I even heard John Geraghty chortling – an appalling noise, I can see why he doesn't do it more often. How on earth would they react if someone cracked a real joke?

I strained, though, to hear Alicia. She was silent.

But not for long.

As the chuckles subsided into weak sighs she piped up, letting her words fall into a vulnerable opening.

'What of her father?'

Once again, strangely, it was John Geraghty who had the courage to respond, his voice thick with contempt.

'He does not deserve a daughter.'

There seemed to be no answer to that, and no one attempted to make one, not even Alicia. He continued, and there was no trace of timidity about him now.

'I went down there and asked about. Not one person had a good word for him. He has been before the magistrate, more than once. Did you know that?' I could not tell whom he was addressing.

'He traps birds. Puts them in cages and sells them in Dublin,' he said. 'And he's a drunk.'

He seemed to realise that he had overstepped the mark, for he stopped and addressed Alicia. 'I'm sorry, Mrs Coote. I shouldn't have jumped in on you like that.'

'It certainly was a surprise,' said Alicia dryly.

'That's the man he is though,' he persisted. 'A criminal. A drunken fool.'

His tone held an unspoken, 'And that's the last I'll say on the matter.'

Footsteps announced the arrival of Sheila. She hesitated, as one who has entered a room and sensed the bad air in it. I wouldn't consider her hugely perceptive, so the pall of awkwardness must have been immense.

'Eh, will I serve the brack?'

'Yes, Sheila,' said Alicia genially. 'I think brack would be the very thing.'

✦

I lingered at the door after our guests departed, listening to the sound of Morrie's powerful Edson rounding the corner and receding. Alicia did not wait with me, and I heard her ambling into the parlour, strangely relaxed in her gait. I both did and did not want to talk to her.

I wonder if it would have made any difference if I had followed her into the debris-strewn table. If I had stood with her for a moment perhaps, companionably, ventured a hand to her soft hair and asked, 'Tell me why you think what we are doing is so wrong.'

I suspect it would have made no difference at all

to the outcome, for I would not have listened to her whatever she said, so excited I was and so *happy*. But it might have thawed the frost that was forming between us if I had reached out to touch her hair and ask her that question.

Seven

Kitty calls me 'a right little lady' for taking breakfast in my room. But she says it with a smile so I know she doesn't really mind. I think Dolas minds, for she never says a word to me and she bangs the tray down on the little table by my window in a cross way.

Nobody pays much attention to what Dolas thinks, though, so I don't either. I think she is jealous of the way everyone in the house is so nice with me.

This morning she was even crosser than usual, and instead of not saying anything she said something nasty instead. When she came in with the tray, I must admit I didn't really notice her. Usually I try to make a sign with my eyes that says 'Hello'.

But today I was sitting on the edge of my bed and taking a big, lovely sniff of the cotton in the night-garment that Kitty bought me. Sometimes I try to imagine what the place is like where the laundry goes, but it reminds me of washdays in the old days and, as Mrs Scallon says, it's best not to dwell on the past.

'Your *ladyship!*'

That was the mean thing that Dolas said to me.

After she had gone I thought about what she had said. I didn't mind that she had said a cross thing, for it is all the same whether you think horrible things or say them out loud. I knew Dolas thought that I was 'above my station', but until now I had never wondered whether I am or not.

I looked about me at the all the lovely things in my room. My room. I thought those words in my head, out loud, as it were: 'My room.'

Kitty always says 'your room', and so does Morrie and Mrs Scallon. Now that I came to think of it, even Dolas said it only the day before when I got butter on the cuff of my blouse: 'Go up to your room and change.'

She never calls me 'Miss' when nobody is about but us.

So it really was my room, and another thing, it really was my blouse as well. I suppose all of the things I have now are mine.

I ate my toast and butter, and it was cold from coming all the way up from the kitchen, but I didn't mind. The bread I eat here comes wrapped up from the shop. Liam once told me that Egan's shop had started to do wrapped up bread, but nobody would buy it. Liam said that it was a waste to buy bread when you could make it, and who would want to buy invisible bread anyway; anything could be wrong with it and a person wouldn't know, and Daddy pushed up his sleeve and opened and closed his fist a couple of times in agreement. I wonder do they buy bread now that there is no one to bake.

The tea they give me smells of flowers. To be perfectly honest I find it a little weak, 'helpless' as Cass used to say, and it comes in tiny little cups that you can hardly scrooch your finger into the handle of. But the cups are pretty, with sprigs of pink and yellow flowers on them, and there is a little silver teapot as well so you can always pour another cup if the need is there.

When I came here first, Mrs Scallon told me all the things I could have for breakfast if I wanted. Don't be talking! It was the funniest thing I had heard for ages. She said a long list of teatime things, and even dinner things that people in Dublin city have for their breakfast. She even mentioned fish and lamb chops. I didn't want to be rude and laugh, so I just opened my eyes very, very wide and that made Mrs Scallon laugh instead.

Then she said would I just like tea and toast and conserve and I nodded 'Yes.'

As it turned out, conserve is another way to say jam.

I missed my morning egg in the beginning, but then I realised that with so much food going on at the other meals it would be foolish to fill up first thing in the morning. Eggs are dead ordinary, really. Another thing was I didn't want to get like Dolas and Mrs Scallon. They wear the same kind of things every day and I hate to say it, about Mrs Scallon anyway, but they never look very nice, for they are both quite fat and it bulges out their clothes. Now that I had such fine clothes, I wanted to show them off well.

Interestingly, I am a different sort of shape here than I was in Shannack, but it's a nicer shape, more like Kitty, but without the tummy. Morrie calls me his 'womanette', and I think myself I look a bit like the bird bath in Cass's back garden, where the Greek lady is carrying a huge shell of water in front of her head as you look at it from the parlour window. She's buck naked except for a flap of a scarf running from her shoulder to her lower parts that shows up all her pretty curves: that's what you get from good food and cleverly arranged garments.

Another thing I have to get used to, being a Dublin girl, is that it takes quite a while to decide what to wear since I have built up quite a collection of clothes in only four months. In Shannack it was just everyday or Sunday, and you didn't have to choose since you can't do anything about the days of the week, can you? Today, though, I took fully ten minutes fingering my things and choosing what I most liked.

After some thought, I selected my three-quarter length burgundy wool skirt, the middle-good cream blouse and I laid the blue long cardigan that goes with my stockinette jumper suit on the bed, in case it got chilly later on. Unfortunately I haven't yet got a cardigan in the burgundy/pink colour range so I resolved to brave it out as long as I could rather than be a holy show, not to tone.

If it got really cold, I could always change into the blue tweed skirt or the jumper suit at a push, but quite frankly I felt the blue tweed didn't come within an ass's roar of the burgundy wool for style, and, realistically, quite *apart* from requiring a complete undergarment change, I could hardly wear stockinette on a Monday morning!

When I had changed into my clothes, I looked at my figure in the mirror. I have a long oval mirror in my room, hinged at the middle in a frame. I have it set so that it just shows me my clothes for the most part, although I can tilt it another way when I want to do my hair or put on a hat.

Kitty has bought me three lovely hats. I think she chose them because they have little veils on them and it makes it easier to go out, but even so, they are beautiful. When I have one of them on me, I look at myself from top to toe and, if I say so myself, I look well. It's nice to know and I think it's a pity that you can't wear a hat when anyone comes to visit the house.

I do love my new hair, though. Kitty insisted on having it shingled, very soon after I came, and she practically had to tie me to the chair, I was so against the idea. I had old-fashioned ideas about long hair, really, but what would you expect with me being still *very* country at that point? But honestly! When I saw the way she had it, with the bangs across my forhead and it bobbed longer at the front than the back, the way you could swing it forward and look over the slant of it with your eyes, I was 'a complete convert' (to quote Kitty!).

I stood over the bed for a little while, fighting with myself to not make it. I still have to struggle every morning to leave it all rumpled, but everybody gets very upset if I do too much upstairs. Now I have to content myself with sleeping very still and slipping out of bed very carefully so as not to make too much of a mess.

For some reason I can do certain things around the house and not others. When I'm in the kitchen with Mrs Scallon and Dolas, I can do any work I please. When I'm upstairs, though, I'm hardly allowed to do anything unless it's to help Kitty, so it gets a little confusing. Once, in the very early days, she caught me carrying my breakfast tray downstairs and she clasped her face between her two hands and leaned it to one side and said 'O!'

She began to laugh then and told me that I was priceless, but she didn't stop me taking the tray down. I wasn't sure if I had done a bad thing and she was just being nice, or if she thought taking the tray was the right thing to do. To be on the safe side, I always sneak down with the tray nowadays.

I was nearly down the good stairs, when I saw the letter.

It was lying on the hall table on top of two other envelopes. In books, when a person gets a shock and they are holding something, the shock makes them drop that thing. I did something different. I clutched the tray very tightly in my hands so that all the china and silver on it rattled. I recognised the writing on it, spelling out Morrie's name and our address: Daddy had written those words.

A desperate thought came to me then. I wanted to throw the tray to the floor and let all the things break. Then I would run over to the hall table, seize the letter and take it up to my room and burn it in my basin, just like I had burned the rags. In my mind's eye I could see the paper ash floating down onto Fitzwilliam Square like snow. I knew the letter could have no good in it, but I could not let go of the tray.

I tried to think clearly. Daddy had gone into the back of my mind, and Liam too. I did not like to think of them, for they seemed like characters in a book I no longer liked. Now I saw and smelled them clearly. I stood at the foot of the good stairs and I could see the light of the fire showing the little white hairs on Daddy's face when he didn't shave. I smelled stale porter from the air in the morning when I came through the kitchen to gather the water pail and the basket for the turf.

I thought about my arms. How they had become roundy and soft in the three months I had been here. The letter seemed to sit hard on the table, and it seemed to me that it made my arms all sinewey again. I had to get away from it.

I rounded the corner and into the little dark passageway that leads to the kitchen stairs. Down I went, still clutching the tray too tightly.

Mrs Scallon was threading lard through a piece of meat with the big cooking needle. She barely looked at me, thanks be to God, but just threw a smile my way without opening her mouth. I set the tray down beside the sink and put on my apron, and it was a relief not to have to worry about rattling the tray. As I scoured the things I stole little glances at her. Watching her calmed me down. It's the same as when I would watch Cass do house things, blowing the fire to life, or pulling apart nettles with her hands in gloves.

Mrs Scallon's hands are plump and red, with a wedding band buried in one finger like a cheese wire. She plunged the needle into the pink flesh and it made a ripping noise as it came out. She did it over and over, and when she had finished I was rinsing the crockery and breathing slowly again.

'Did that little rip brown you?' she commented after a while.

I had no idea what she meant, as I don't understand the Dublin language mostly. Mrs Scallon is harder to understand even than Dolas, for she speaks in Dublin, but the voice she speaks it in is posh, so the sounds are *very* odd. I must have had a puzzled look on me for she went on.

'She'd a face on her like a penn'orth of puddin' in a paper bag after getting you the breakfast. Looked like she'd been riz, but, sure you'd riz nottin'.'

And she said no more, but set to plumping the meat down on a spiked plate and scrubbing down the table like it was the deck of a ship, with two hands on the scouring brush.

I went mooching off hunting for the glass cloths, with no more clue what she had said than if a monkey had spoken to me, but I didn't worry for a second. You see, Mrs Scallon always talks like that: in bursts. Its very nice, for it's not like having a conversation. I think she just talks to keep her hand in, like touching a smoothing iron with a wet finger, just to check it's still hot, but not to actually iron anything.

We worked on together, although we did different things. I can choose the things I do here instead of having to do everything, which is a great happiness to me. One of the things I like to do is to wash and prepare the vegetables and garden things, because it reminds me of Cass. It suits Mrs Scallon, because what she likes to do best of all is to get at the meat.

You can't imagine the amount of meat Dublin people eat. Mostly we used to just have pig things: trotters and cheeks and ears and rashers and sausage, and not even every day. Or hen things, obviously. But in Morrie and Kitty's house they eat everything that trots, scampers, flies or swims. I am only learning the names for all of them; my head is dizzy with it! Venison and turbot and briskets and crab and lobster and Sir Loins and scallops and quails and kippers and roll mops and pheasants.

I sometimes say the names out loud when I'm on my own, in a bouncy rhythm, like a march, and I like to add a new name every time. My favourite name at the moment is roll mops: '*ROLL* mops! *ROLL* mops! *ROLL* mops! *ROLL* mops!'

I think that brains are in the flesh of things, for Dublin people are all terribly clever. Daddy and Liam are not brainy at all, I would say, and probably that comes from mostly eating pigs. I am glad that I have all that good meat inside me now; it will probably come in useful when I am beautiful. Although Kitty says that beauty is better than brains because men can see better than they can think, but I *think* that's a joke.

'You're to go up to Mrs Halpin after the lunch,' said Mrs Scallon, out of nowhere.

I got a bit of a fright then, but then I remembered — and I think it was quite clever of me to work this out so quickly — that Mrs Scallon and I had been in the kitchen ever since I saw the letter, so if Kitty had already told her she wanted me up after lunch it *couldn't* be about that. Down there for dancing! So I just kept snipping the tops off the beans.

❀

When Dolas brought the lunch things down, I took off my apron and smoothed out my clothes. I could see that she had a puss on her so I didn't look at her straight for I wouldn't give her the satisfaction, quite frankly. Off I stalked, leaving her to stew in her own juices.

Actually, I'm always a little nervous going upstairs. I don't know why because I always have a lovely time and I nearly always get given something new. It's just that maybe I feel more comfortable when I have things to do. Upstairs I feel a little bit like I'm in one of my daydreams but I'm not in charge or something. Or maybe it's just that I get all excited.

I hurried up to Kitty's study and I knocked on the door in a fluttery way because I was very wound up.

'Is that my little Veronica?' said Kitty's voice, like she was singing.

I didn't answer but I came through the door and I lowered my head so that my bob fell forward and she could see that my eyes were smiling. I always feel like a pixie when I do that.

'O! Little darling!' she said delightedly, her eyes gleaming, and I was glad that I had put the right look on me. 'Come! Come! Come and let me show you the lovely things I have for you!'

A pile of rectangular boxes were in front of her, and a round one on the french escritoire, and the strings that had kept them shut were cut with a scissors that was lying on top of the biggest box. I felt spit coming into my mouth as if I was looking at a delicious meal and the spit was hot around my tongue.

She pointed her finger and let it roam from the floor boxes, and then slowly up to the round box and back to the floor. Then, as she crept her finger back up towards the escritoire, she said in a rush, 'What would you say to a scrumptious *hat*?', and I swear to God I had to jam my hand against my mouth against the laughing, for the words came into my head.

'Hel-lo HAT!'

'You see! I know my Veronica!' said Kitty, thrilled. She must have thought my smile was because of the hat, which of course it was.

She opened the round box, very slowly, looking right into my eyes the whole time. Out of the box came a shape, covered in thin paper, which rustled. She teased the paper off and the hat sat on her fist like it was in the window of a shop. It was, as Kitty would say, simply divine.

It was made of pale straw, and it was obviously a big round hat, but it was made long and thin by a sky blue ribbon that pulled down the sides of it and tied where a person's chin would be. There was no veil to it, but I could see that the long front of it would shade a person's face.

The nicest part of it was that around the brim were false flowers. They were like no flowers that I had ever seen, but I wished I could see real ones like them. They were shaped like the flowers that Cass calls Ragged Robin, but instead of being pink like sweets they were the same pale blue as the satin ribbon. They were as real looking as if they were real.

I reached out for the hat without even thinking about it. I put it on me and let the ribbon caress my neck. I wanted to see myself.

But Kitty said, 'Now try this!' and she opened a box that was as long as a coffin almost. There was more rustly paper in that box and out of it she took – a dress.

It was the most perfect dress in the world. I knew this dress, for I had worn it a thousand times in my dreams. It took my breath away.

It was blue like the ribbon on my lovely hat and it had little white stripes running down it from the neck to the end of it. The skirt of it started where your hips are and it was shaped around the waist where a woman goes in. The neckline had a shallow frill to it, but it scooped right down into the front of the dress almost as low as a man's shirt front! If another person had showed me that neckline I would have thought them impertinent, but I was very glad that Kitty had bought me that dress.

I shed my skirt and blouse like they were mere rags that I hated. Kitty had her hands together in front of her face like she was praying, but she had a smile on her that nobody has when they pray.

I put on the dress.

Kitty's study has mirrors in it. In fact all of Kitty's rooms have lots of mirrors and it can be very difficult. This time, however, I was glad of the mirrors. When I had buttoned all the many buttons at the front of the dress I turned to the longest mirror in the room.

I lowered my head so I could just see out from under the brim of my hat. A gentle, sweet girl looked back at me. I turned my foot out as I had seen Kitty do and lifted my head a fraction so you could see my bob, and the sweet girl turned just a little bit naughty; I looked the very picture of a little 'flapper', just *asking* for trouble.

Actually, it was hard to strike the balance between keeping the hat low enough to maintain the illusion and high enough so I didn't look like a dress wearing a hat, but I managed it.

'Veronica,' said Kitty, quietly. I turned around to her, though, to be honest, I didn't really want to look away from my image in the mirror.

I thought she was going to say how beautiful I looked in my new dress and hat, but she didn't.

'Can you keep a secret?' she said.

I am the very best person to keep a secret, for I keep all the things that are in my head a secret every single minute of the day. I nodded very hard, and the hat nodded even more than my head and ended up in front of my face entirely, and bang went the illusion! I heard Kitty's lovely bubbling laugh, and I was laughing myself as I lifted it back to where it belonged.

She looked so happy that I knew that the secret must be something wonderful and I was beside myself with excitement wondering what was going to come next. But before she could tell me what it was, there was a sharp knocking on the door of the room, and the next thing she said was, 'Come.'

Dolas opened the door and stood there looking at me in my finery. Now I was sure that she was jealous of me, for she had a real face on her.

'Yes, Dolas?' said Kitty. She never used her nice voice with Dolas and a mean part of me was glad of that.

'Dr Geraghty is in the parlour. He wants to speak to you and … Veronica.'

She said my name as if it hurt her to say it. Kitty snapped back at her: '*Miss Broderick.*'

Dolas looked like she couldn't believe her ears, but she had no choice, so she said, 'Miss Broderick. Sorry, ma'am.' She put a smile on her that was as hard as a cauliflower stalk, swivelled around on one foot and left the room.

I waited to see what Kitty would say, and a thousand different thoughts were going on in my head.

I was sure that Dolas would be even more horrible to me after this, for Kitty had shamed her in front of me and she must be feeling very vexed indeed. And she could hardly dare blame Kitty.

Then there was Dr Geraghty.

I always liked his visits, for he seemed to be different with me than with anyone else, more relaxed. That made me feel quite special, even though he was just a doctor visiting.

I think, though, he liked seeing me as well. Maybe a person who has got very muddy and hysterical with someone feels more at ease if they know that person will never tell.

Kitty turned to me and said in a breathy little voice, '*You* go down to him, Veronica.'

I froze looking at her. There was something in her voice that made me feel as if too much was being asked of me. I thought that I should do something or say something, so I made a quizzical face and Kitty said, 'Go down and talk to your beau!' And she laughed her lovely laugh again, but this time I didn't like it.

I wanted to ask her to come with me, for I hadn't been alone with Dr Geraghty since those two times in Shannack, and I didn't see any need for it now.

'I'll be just behind you!' she said then, so I had to do what she had asked.

I walked out of the room and went down the stairs towards the parlour.

I was glad that I was wearing such nice stuff, but I didn't know what to do about the hat, so I just left it on my head. The parlour door was open, and as I stood in the doorway, I could see him looking out the windows to the garden. I noticed the slices of flesh at his wrists where his suit was too short for him; you'd think a doctor would be able to buy a nice suit for himself.

I nearly always know when another person has come into a room even if I'm not looking at them. The air sort of changes. Nobody ever hears me coming in, though, because I have a light tread out of habit. I decided not to clear my throat to let him know, and just observed him instead.

He's a very fidgety person when there are people around, so I was surprised at how still he was on his own. He stared out the window and didn't move a muscle, stiller even than an ordinary person. I wondered what was going through his mind.

I suddenly remembered that Kitty was following me, so I realised that I would have to cough after all as it would look very peculiar if she came down and I had not announced myself.

He turned around.

He said nothing to begin with, but just looked at me in a curious way that made me feel hot.

'I hope I'm not holding you up,' he said.

I was puzzled, until I realised that I was dressed nearly for the outdoors. A person in their dress and hat is only lacking a coat. I shook my head to let him know that he was not holding me up.

'I was coming to see Kitty anyway, so I thought I would give you the good news in person,' he said.

I wondered what business he had with Kitty, but I didn't give much room to that thought because I wanted to concentrate on the good news. I was so excited I could hardly bear it, for you see I knew well what he was going to say.

'We haven't nailed it down to the day yet, but your operation will certainly be sometime next week.' He had a kindly look on his face as he went on. 'Best thing would be to pack a little bag next Monday, that way you'll be ready as soon as word comes.'

It seemed to me that the room, and everything in it, went white at that moment. My body felt weak and I felt a jolt inside me where my legs meet. I had hardly dared to hope about the operation, even though I knew in my heart that Morrie and Kitty were trying to make it happen, but sometimes I would stand among the bluebells, so to speak, and travel through all the moments of my life in beauty. Now that Dr Geraghty had said the words, I was overwhelmed.

Some of it was happiness, of course it was, but some of it was fear. I hadn't forgotten, you see. The letter was still sitting on the table like a sea crow.

What if Daddy was going to take me back there? What if he was on his way, even now, to make me go back on the train? Tears filled my eyes and I started to tremble at the thought that my beauty might be snatched from me when it was now so very, very close.

Without warning, Dr Geraghty moved towards me, and before I could do anything about it he had put his arms right around me and he held me against his clothes. I didn't pull away from him because I was so shocked. Nobody had ever held me in what you might call a 'hug' before. Tears poured down my face and as I shook with the sudden force of them, his arms tightened around me and he said, 'Don't fret, Veronica. You'll be fast asleep for the whole thing. It will be fine.'

His words made me think, and that stopped the crying. A person cannot think and cry at the same time, for crying is an animal thing.

Of course, he could never have known the reason for my tears. It amazed me that he would think I was afraid of the operation and I realised that he didn't know me at all. Well, how could he?

I breathed out a great sigh, and when I breathed in again I got the smell of him real strong. He didn't smell damp this time.

I liked his smell, and as I breathed in again I decided that I preferred it even to the smell of Morrie's cologne.

It was kind of comfortable just standing there

with my head lying against his chest, breathing in the warm man-smell of him. Just as I was starting to think I should move away from him, I heard a voice from the doorway.

'O! *Well*, perhaps I should have knocked!' Kitty spoke in a knowing sort of voice.

Naturally, we sprang apart.

I was embarrassed to be caught in such a private moment and I wished that Kitty *had* knocked. But when I looked at Dr Geraghty and heard him speak, I realised that my embarrassment was a tiny thing compared to his. His face had great beet-rooty blotches on it and when he addressed Kitty he kept his eyes on his shoes.

'Eh ... she ... Veronica was upset. I'm ... I ... she was crying ... I just ...'

'O, John! You don't need to explain,' she interrupted gaily. 'I think it is charming of you to take such *particular* care of your little patient.'

I could hear Dr Geraghty breathing in and out in a way that sounded almost angry. When he spoke again, his voice was rather tight.

'I came to see that all is well with you, Mrs Halpin, and to give you some news.'

As Dr Geraghty told her about the operation and the little bag I was to have ready on Monday, I wondered again what his business with Kitty could be. She assured him that she was 'absolutely in the pink!' and Dr Geraghty made his goodbyes and left. He did not look at me again.

'I suppose you can guess my little secret now. Hmm?' said Kitty, smiling. I suddenly realised that she was terribly excited, for her eyes were gleaming and I wished that I *could* guess what her secret was.

I felt very stupid so I decided to do a bad thing and dissemble. I nodded my head and tried to look as excited as she.

'Yes,' she said solemnly. 'I'm sure you will be the very best companion any little one could have,' and she ran her hand over her belly and I knew.

I kept smiling as best I could, for I couldn't let on that I had not understood her at first. But inside I was in a heap.

Every night, before I closed my eyes, I imagined how my life would be when I was beautiful. Now I saw another picture in my mind: walking through Fitzwilliam Square pushing a perambulator, a baby that was not mine.

I felt no rush in my stomach when I thought about this. I had got used to being the special person in the house and I did not want it to change, now that my heart's desire was so close. No.

Kitty was talking again. I half heard her saying nice things about how men would be throwing themselves at me after the operation, how I would be the very *belle*, but most of my mind was making plans.

I would have to find other imaginings to make my stomach rush and jolts happen. I felt a little like when I used to stand among the bluebells in Shannack Woods, wishing.

Now, however, I was not content to wish. The difference between wishing and wanting is that when you want something you make plans to get it. I started to think about what I wanted.

The front door slammed and Kitty said, 'Ah! The man himself. Let's tell him your good news, Veronica.'

We heard Morrie bellowing.

'*Kit!*'

We hurried into the hall. Morrie was standing by the little table, holding Daddy's note in his hand. He looked up at us and his face was not gay as it usually is. He looked down at the paper and he read aloud the words on it: 'Bring Veronica to Séipéal Naomh Deirbhile in Shannack on Wednesday at ten o'clock for her brother's wedding.'

Wednesday was the day after tomorrow.

Eight

Morrie had promised that we would drive down, but at the last minute the Hillman got banjaxed and nobody could fix it in time. Then Kitty and Morrie had a big row, with Kitty saying that they couldn't possibly go down *there* in the Edson, it would be rubbing everyone's noses in it. Morrie protested that they'd always driven down in the past, but Kitty had an answer for him.

'Yes, angel, but we always took the *worst* car.'

I always thought their cars looked grand. I must make it my business to find out what's a good car and what's a worst car, for you could get caught out badly there.

I was terribly disappointed, for there is nearly nothing I like to do so much as be in Morrie's motor cars, even the kitten one. Well, except for when Kitty is driving, and you think you're going to be killed. I thought, somehow, I might be in a more cheery mood if we'd just all had a lovely motor car outing.

Then, I was afraid we would be late, for Kitty decided on the last possible train, that would only get us there by a squeak. Even though I didn't want to get there at all, I wished we could have got the earlier train, but as Kitty said, 'What on earth would we do in Shannack if we got there early?'

She said it to Morrie, and he fully agreed with her, but the truth was that I didn't want to draw down notice on us.

I hated the train journey. It made me feel sick because it was like going up to Dublin but the other way around.

When I went up to Dublin all those months ago my excitement grew with everything that I saw. Everything seemed so open and free; sheep whooshing over the low hills like God had a giant broom and was sweeping their woolly bodies through the fields. Enormous flocks of crows scattering upwards from the massive fields at the noise of the train, making the sky dark for an instant.

I saw rich people's farms with acres and acres and *acres* stretching away behind huge square houses with ivy tumbling down from the roofs, and I saw dinky madey-up little farmhouses, that I thought at that time I would like to live in. They looked like someone had thrown wooden blocks out of a bag and a family just moved into them as they lay, and filled them with cattle and dogs and pigs and children. They were mad looking!

I saw the mossy stone bridges over rushy rivers, and I peeped over my shawl at the fashionable ladies at the stations, snuggling tawny-coloured furs and clopping about in heels. The nearer I got to Dublin, the more fashionable some of them got, although some of them got poorer too. By the time I got to Harcourt Street Station, everyone looked either dog-rough, or as if they were friends with the King of England!

Now I saw each station and bridge and farm again, but each of them was bringing me closer to Shannack and Daddy. I wondered would it be better never to have seen the world and all the beautiful things in it if you had to go back to where everything is ugly, and to only remember it all.

After a while I had to stop looking out of the window, it was making me so miserable, and I tried to listen to Morrie and Kitty chatting. Normally I love to hear the easy way they are with each other. This time, though, I just felt ill.

My new boots crunched on the gravel outside the church. It was a place I had never been before, for we always went to the Church of the Holy Ghost. This must be the Puddie church. It was quite close to the station, but I had never, ever been there. There was nobody outside it so I knew we must be 'running late'. Kitty touched my hand as we came to the door and I stopped and looked up at them both. They smiled at me in a worried kind of way and I felt a kind of a surge inside.

'You look beautiful,' Kitty said.

My cheeks got hot and I felt a kind of courage come into me, for indeed I knew that my outfit was fit for anywhere.

Kitty must be a mind reader, for the very next thing she got me after the dress was a beautiful wool, burgundy, three-quarter length cardigan. She followed that up with an ankle length assymetric burgundy coat with saucer-sized buttons to it, just five of them, and, of course, I knew she wouldn't let me down in the head department, and so what next do you think? Burgundy felt, veiled, feathered and blackberried: The Hat to end all Hats. Vacancy filled. No other hats need apply.

Thinking about my things made me feel *much* less mousey. As I *looked* up at them, Morrie, handsome in his light suit and silk cravatte, and Kitty, *divine* in fireweed pink, I felt I belonged between them. I looked like I belonged between them, and there was no way on God's earth I was going to come back here to this pigsty to work like a black slave! I decided that there was nothing wrong with a sister calling down to see her brother getting married and meet her in-laws. Nothing at all odd about a daughter that's come up in the world coming back to see her old father.

I led them into the church at a lick.

We stopped inside the door and took in the scene. Everybody was facing the altar so we could look at them all for a moment in peace. The right-hand side of the church was stuffed with people, but there was something very peculiar about the make-up of them. I had never seen so many fat ladies before, and each of them seemed to be with a thin man. It was like a rule. Even the old men on the right-hand side of the church were beside fat old ladies. I hadn't seen any of them before so they must all be Puddie's. I heard Kitty murmur, 'Good God!'

And I knew why she said it. The ladies on the Puddie side, as well as being enormous, were wearing an enormous amount of clothes. I have learned something about fashion from Kitty and I did *not* think that the Puddie ladies were at all fashionable. I tried to pick out exactly what mistake they were making, and it occurred to me that when a person is large it is not a good idea for them to wear frills.

I was so distracted by the Puddies, and my own vain thoughts about clothes, that I had forgotten about why I was there. When I looked over to the other side of the church my thoughts stilled and a sadness came into my heart; there were just seven people there.

I saw the back of Cass, and beside her a dark woman. It must have been her daughter Brigid from Dublin, for she stood very close to her, but I could not see her face. A few seats in front of them were Moss and May Egan from the shop. We didn't know them very well and they had never been to the house.

Two men were in front of them. They wore work trousers and jackets that didn't go. One of them was small and wiry and I had seen him before. His name was Páidi and he worked alongside Liam on the farms. I remembered Liam telling me that Páidi was an innocent, which means that he talks to himself all the time and swipes at his eyes in an odd way, but Liam says he is a good worker. I didn't know the other man from the back, but he must have been another labourer, for they are the only people that Liam knows. Alfie Hoey maybe or Orange Pete. It didn't really matter.

In front of the men was Daddy.

Kitty touched my shoulder, and we three made our way to a bench at the back of the church and sat down. People on the Puddie side started to notice us and they looked around curiously. It was as if each person drew another person around with them, and very soon it seemed as if the whole church was looking over their shoulders at us. All but Daddy.

Liam was standing at the centre of the church in front of the altar. He was wearing his best suit that didn't fit him any more, and he looked uncomfortable. When he saw me he gazed across the wide space between us and his eyes were like a deer: full of feeling.

He put his hand to his chest and he lifted the fingers towards me, and I knew he was admiring my fine clothes and appearance. His chest went up and down like he was sighing and I felt a thrill of pride that he should be so moved by seeing me. Then he gave an uneasy glance at the door of the church and something dark came across his face and he turned back to the altar. I thought he looked very sad for a bridegroom.

Still Daddy did not turn around.

A loud noise made us all jump. Kitty actually made a little scream, but only someone close beside her could have heard it over the din. I recognised the sound of a church organ, but I had never heard one so loud and so ill-tuned. I heard Morrie groaning and then both Kitty and Morrie started to make giggling noises, which they tried to stifle. All eyes on the Puddie side turned to the back of the church, and they had an expression on them like when a person is happily expecting to hear the punchline of a joke.

I glanced over at Liam. He, too, was looking to the door, but he looked like someone who has stepped into a field and realised that it has a bull in it.

I saw Cass's face, shrewd and curious, and beyond hers I saw the back of Daddy. He had not turned around. We were the only two people in the church looking forward, and I was looking at him and I knew that he was only thinking of me.

Old feelings came to me, things I had not felt or thought about for months. I felt again the little bits and pieces of care and concern I had had for him: looking at him asleep by the fire and wishing that he would go up to his bed where he could get proper rest, wanting him to eat his dinner before he went to Tubridy's, waiting for a little grunt from him that would make me know he was pleased with me. Wanting him to say some little, affectionate thing to me.

'Your mother wore her hair like that.'

I heard those words in my mind and my heart swelled; I wanted him to turn and look at me.

A gasp from the Puddie side and a muffled 'Jesus, Mary and Holy Saint Joseph!' from Kitty announced the arrival of Molly Puddie.

I turned my head away from Daddy, reluctantly, for I wished to the last that he would turn around like everybody else.

She stood in the doorway on the arm of an exhausted-looking man who must have been her father. Tears sprang up into my eyes.

She was hideous.

She wore a huge white gown that looked like it had been piped out of an icing bag by a person with an unsteady hand. Above the dress sat her face, like an overstuffed cushion, and although everything else about her was full and bulging, her mean mouth ran across her face like a line made with the thin side of a piece of chalk. I *hated* her.

She was not as beautiful as a flower, not even the meanest knotgrass that arrests a farmer's harrow. She looked exactly as she had sounded from behind the railway station door: rude and ugly.

I whipped around to look at my father's back. Now I saw only the creases in his suit and a faint greyness of dirt on the back of his neck. I knew what was going on.

I threw my gaze over to the Puddies with their expensive clothes and bad taste, and I looked at my brother at the head of the church, dying quietly inside his great big man's body.

Daddy had sold Liam to this creature for her farm.

It was all wrong.

The very pinnacle and reward of life is marriage and love. Only beauty deserved such a prize and this pig had beauty in no part of her. A panic rose up in me as I realised that she was going to attach herself to my kind brother as goosegrass clings to a person who is innocently walking the fields.

'*You'll do no better, so don't think you will!*'

Those words rang around my head and my hands made themselves into fists. If I were not his sister *I* would have kept house for Liam and loved him. He would have done better and Daddy must have known it, for *he* got Mammy when everybody said she was going way beneath herself.

I looked up and, like a bad dream, I saw a priest on the altar in front of the pair of them, like he'd just appeared out of thin air. He was tall and he had a lot of moles on his face, and when he spoke his voice was quite swanky for Shannack. He started to say words from the mass and the air got heavy with seriousness.

I wanted to shout out and stop it all, but the words went on – clack, clack – like the wheels of a train.

Because I could not do anything except rage, I contented myself with boring my gaze into the back of Daddy's neck. As the priest clackety-clacked on, I wished boils onto my father's neck, painful as the droning voice, I was so ragingly angry.

I looked over to the Puddies' side and I picked apart every little gesture and ruffle and bulge. I felt like a witch cursing everyone in the church and liking it. Loving my fury. It seemed to me that my rage was so enormous and loud inside me that it was odd that the sacrament didn't stop because of it. I felt my own silence more than I ever had before.

I imagined what it would be like if I could shout out all the things I was thinking.

All the fat faces would turn around to me and listen, horrified. Liam would walk off somewhere into the air and be free and Molly Puddie would be crushed with shame and wish she were me with my neat body and my fine clothes and my dignity.

Her dress would melt into her body like a molten shoe and cause her excruciating pain and she would beg me for water to harden it, but I would refuse. And Daddy would weep and reach his arms out to me to give me a hug.

But the fat faces looked adoringly at the sow, and Liam stayed standing by her side, and the priest said, 'Do you, Liam Broderick, take this woman to be your lawful, wedded wife? Will you love and cherish her, and take her for richer, for poorer, in sickness and in health, until death do you part?'

There was a silence, just the length of an intake of breath, and Liam said in a tight voice, 'I do,' and my heart went down deep into me where it was hard to find it.

I tried to find some place inside me where I didn't have to listen any more. I closed my eyes and I strained to hear anything that was beyond the open door of the church. At first I could hear only a bird twittering in the trees of the churchyard. It was not my bird, for its call was confused and jittery. Some little brown bird, maybe.

Then, as I concentrated harder, thirsty for peace, I could hear other sounds. A cow lowing in a far field; a clop of distant hooves with wheels rattling behind them.

Then tinier noises: a rustle of leaves, and the very air itself I heard, moving over the land. I had forgotten those sounds living in the great city. Country sounds, I suppose they are, but they were soothing to me and they let my mind still and my heart come back to me a little.

Suddenly, a terrible din started up in the church – somebody had started playing the organ again, and I opened my eyes and I saw that the wedding was over.

Molly and Liam had turned around and were starting to walk to the door of the church. The Puddies were smiling and making cooing pidgeoney noises that you could just hear under the wrong notes that the organ was playing. Molly had a tight look on her fat face and I nearly snorted for noticing that she looked like she had three pairs of breasts one under another.

I saw Liam's face, though, and that stopped my mirth. When he came close to me he put a brave smile on him and gave me one of his affectionate, watery looks. Molly had her arm clamped around his and she soon swept him past me, and left me looking only at a line of Puddies.

People were filing out of the church, starting with the ones from the front. But I couldn't see anyone I knew yet. After more Puddies came past, I saw Cass. She was wearing an odd black dress with beads of jet on it. It looked like a dress you would wear in your coffin, but Cass is not that interested in fashion. She caught my gaze and she looked curious. My veil was thick, and it seemed as if she was wondering what was going on in my mind. I was glad that she couldn't know.

Moss's red face passed, grinning to no one in particular. I knew that May would be beside him, but she is a short person and she was hidden from me by Puddies.

I saw him then.

He trailed the rest of the company, and he was looking straight ahead. As he came towards where we were sitting he stumbled slightly and he stopped to regain himself. I was staring at him as if I had never seen him before. He was a couple of benches in front of us and he did not continue, but stayed where he was. Very slowly, he turned his head around and his eyes picked me out and looked at me. He looked almost as if he was afraid.

Then a terrifying thing happened. My Daddy's eyes filled up with tears, and they rolled down his cheeks with no one to dry them.

He stood there for what seemed like a long time. I could not do anything to help him though, for I found that beneath my veil my eyes were dry. I let him stand there for as long as he would, and then I watched him leave the church and follow his son and his son's new bride.

I knew what to do then.

I turned to Kitty and Morrie and they were looking at me with concern. There was a little door at the altar end of the church and I had noticed before that it led out to the sunshine.

I pointed to it with my arm held straight in front of me, and I walked out in front of them towards it.

Nine

When I was a small boy, there were the astonishing days, the astounding days.

In the summer of my eighth year, when the bluebells had disappeared from the forest floor and the air became drowsy with the scent of meadowsweet, an intolerable excitement took over me. The bass season beckoned and for only the second time ever, I would accompany my father to the sea.

Every morning after breakfast, I entered his study like a jewel thief and lifted the baize cover from the fly-cabinet. My eyes drank in their intricate structures, as familiar to me as living creatures.

Not daring to touch them, I imagined their weight-less forms on my palm, and pictured my hand clenching over them so that the barbed hooks bit into my flesh.

At last, one gorgeous morning in May, my father came into the breakfast room carrying the two rods, dust still clinging to their leather shafts.

'Time to set these to work again, Edward,' he said. 'Quickly, don't dilly-dally.'

That was a day of frantic preparation. The pre-ferred hooks and lures were plucked from the oak cabinet and packed in the leather travelling case for use. Soon we would stand together on the shore at Ceanntrá, my father and I, and cast them into the preposterous, exhilarating water.

✿

I had woken early this morning, and I lay listening to Alicia's open-mouthed snores with a smile on my face.

The last few days had been hugely frustrating, waiting for theatre, surgeon and team to be free at the one time. Morrie told me that the sight of the child's travelling bag still waiting by the front door was making him 'fill up' every time he left the house. What a peculiar specimen he is.

I reached for the clock by my bedside and ran my fingers over the dial: twenty past four. Unable to sleep two nights ago, I had risen at five, and Alicia spent the rest of the day surreptitiously ringing my colleagues to enquire about the symptoms of dementia. She forgets I have excellent hearing.

So I lay in the bed rigid, like the schoolboy I once was, waiting for permission to throw off the covers and embrace the day.

Throughout that morning I was conscious of rushing through the moments. I dressed clumsily and ate my breakfast without savouring the tastes as I should have done. We are such hasty creatures. Of late, I have come to despise the man who runs through life, missing the point. It is in savouring the steps that we taste the essence of things.

I hardly remember getting to the hospital, except for one detail: just before she helped me into the taxi-cab, as she bolstered my collar, my wife pressed her face to mine and lingered for a moment. She had not done that for years.

I smelled the powder from her cheek, and, in my excitement, I did not inquire what that touch meant. I was merely moved by it. That you can be moved by something you do not understand is simply axiomatic. To omit to investigate it, though, is a kind of negligence.

Reggie Sweetman and a nurse greeted me at Sir Patrick Dun's. I shrugged off both arms in an impatient way. I was offended by the amount of support offered for the ten stone steps that I could easily negotiate. I was even more put out by the murmurs of admiration that greeted my attaining the door. But I stifled my fury and let a thin smile seep over my face. I had many favours to repay.

I no longer had rooms of my own in the hospital and I was momentarily unsure as to where I should go. I hesitated in the great doorway, frustrated at my own lack of purpose, and I had to wait for the nurse to direct me to Sweetman's rooms in her soft, country brogue. The voice was familiar to me. I must have looked at her eyes above a white mask a hundred times, but she blended with all the others in my memory.

'It's a great privilege to have you back, sir,' she said in a quiet voice. I rather wished she had said it louder, for Sweetman was striding noisily on the flags before us and I was sure he would not have heard the compliment. In my dealings with him over the past month, he had never given me any indication that he was aware of my stature; although undoubtedly an able surgeon, he struck me as arrogant.

Sweetman's suite smelled of leather, good pipe tobacco and sweat, the very cliché of a man's arena. The nurse touched my arm and led me to a leather chair that bucked alarmingly under me, making me lose my balance for a moment. Another minor humiliation.

'Nurse,' he said curtly, dismissing her.

When the door had closed behind her there was a silence. I directed my gaze ahead of me, disadvantaged by the strange diluted nature of his presence. Just as I began to suspect that he had left the room along with the nurse, I was thunder-struck to hear a familiar, reedy voice.

'Professor Coote.'

John Geraghty was in the room. I was in the company of two men entirely lacking in any kind of physical presence. It was turning into a séance.

When Sweetman finally spoke he was directly behind me. I had an image in my mind of the two of them tiptoeing around me, stifling giggles and putting their fingers to their lips. I longed for a reason to stand up, and I tried to look comfortable in the chair, which I now ascertained was actually on springs. I was starting to hate the power-crazed bastard.

'I want to discuss a matter of *protocol* with you, Professor Coote,' he said, and my throat almost closed over with rage. His dominant position and supercilious tone implied that I had been *summoned* to his chambers. Some sort of reply seemed expected, but I gave him none. I would not let him unman me in front of a fool like Geraghty.

'I say this with the greatest *respect*—' he began, but the superciliousness of his tone shattered my resolve and I could not let him finish. I knew exactly which 'protocol' he wished to propose, to whit: Reginald Sweetman is the King of the Castle, all others bow down before him. I decided to checkmate him.

'If you are about to speak with great respect,' I said, firmly, 'let that respect be for the extraordinary opportunity that has been afforded you.'

I had caught him on the hop for he failed to interrupt me as I had done him. I pressed home my advantage.

'If you are about to patronise me by attempting to delineate a hierarchy of command, then I will say one thing to you.' I stopped, savouring my command of the exchange. 'The only thing of importance today is Veronica Broderick.'

A sudden image in my mind of Alicia fainting to the floor with shock almost punctured the solemnity of the moment. It ameliorated my rage and when next I spoke, I was conscious of myself as an incorrigible chancer.

'If you have anything further to say,' I continued, 'examine it for infection by your own ego and then proceed.'

I heard Sweetman coming around from behind me and coming to rest in a chair, presumably behind his desk. I held my gaze, certain this time that I was meeting his eyes. I could feel his presence now. John Geraghty actually sucked in a breath and, with an illusionist's flourish, the two of them were revealed to me. I was back in control.

At length, Sweetman spoke, this time in a voice that pleased me.

'Professor Coote,' he said with a smile, 'I am starting to understand this hospital's infatuation with you!'

I allowed my eyebrows to raise in a modest way, but I was too hasty; he was merely changing tack.

'I am delighted to hear you express such modern sentiments,' he continued casually, laughing even. 'The day of the brilliant, pioneering, ego-driven surgeon is over, is it not?'

I declined to answer, sensing the direction he was taking, but almost unable to believe my ears. He went on, 'We work as a *team* nowadays, of course. But I'm sure you witnessed enough of that kind of gory showmanship at Gallipoli, I know I did. The rapaciousness of those men! Picking through those poor squaddies like hawkers at a quayside, scrabbling for the best cuts. By Christ! I was only a lowly intern myself, but I'll never forget the *butchery* I saw.'

His tone changed once more, became softer. 'I'm sorry, Professor Coote, I'm clearly bringing back upsetting memories. You were there: it should come as no surprise to find you in favour of the modern, patient-centred approach. I'm sure you were one of the good ones.'

I could not speak. I was prepared to be outmaneuvered, but I had no defences against this *sadism*. Cloaking his vileness in a compliment, the man had just desecrated the memory of every young man I had saved or lost.

I *was* a brilliant, pioneering surgeon – no ego involved – it was an unasked for gift that I often begged the Almighty to take from me, the responsibility so drowned my capacity for joy. What he mistook for ego was something far more rare: courage.

It is not ego that makes a man turn his face from a dying soldier to saw the limb from another who just might live. They were numberless, the frightened, agonised young men who could, without question, have been saved by a *team*. Some months I laboured with a blunt scalpel.

An image that had haunted me for years flooded into my mind once more: another failure. A young soldier who would not be returning to his sweetheart. I could still recall the grim aftermath of our efforts to save his life; the blood which soaked his cut clothing as if he had drowned in gore; the strewn instruments; the gathering flies. The image that haunted me, though, were the woollen socks that peeped over the top of his splattered boots: they did not match. He did not expect to meet his maker when he pulled on one green sock and one grey.

For every one of those young men I would have wished the time and the skill we were going to lavish on this Veronica Broderick. And that coward would have me a butcher.

I felt a hand touch my shoulder and I started. A woman's soft voice said, 'Sir, they've gone. They told me to come in and fetch you.'

✿

Metal resounded off metal in the echoing chamber of the operating theatre. The room sounded full and yet sparse in the way that a bathroom does.

Scrubbed surfaces threw random words brightly forth from the murmuring, as incongruous as sequins glinting on stone flags. They transformed the familiar noises of preparation into something brittle and jagged.

I had planned to conduct a meticulous review of the technical aspects of the surgery we were about to perform, envisioning, somehow, a moment to take command of the proceedings. I had deluded myself. They all knew what they were doing.

There is a perversity in me, I will freely admit, and it made a fool of me. I had considered myself to be a significant member of this ensemble: after all, I had devised this procedure and had pulled every string I still had to get this crack team together to help the child. Now, however, I was functionless, like a fiction writer sneaking into his readers' homes to poke them when they get to the best bits.

The theatre gradually filled again with footsteps and clattering and hushed chat. I had nothing to do. I distracted myself by making knowledgeable inquiries of anyone who came into my purview and dispensing such advice as the time allowed.

What I repeatedly imparted to them, however, was this: her name.

As I chatted to them about this and that, I used the child's name again and again, personalising her to them in the hope that it would make their efforts greater. Perhaps in the back of my mind were all the nameless youngsters I had selected for salvation or for death.

But something else was happening as I named her. Like Dante, immortalising his beloved, every 'Veronica Broderick' I gave to the assembled team was a gently whispered '*Alicia*.'

After a space, I found myself next to Moynihan, the anaesthetist, and I attempted to converse with him, with little success. Such a dull and taciturn fellow! Where the next generation of charismatic practitioners is to come from is, to steal from Dickens, a 'deep and sealed mystery'.

'Of course, the first anaesthetist was Our Lord himself,' I said.

'Yes,' he replied, stonewalling me.

He was not the only person in the room, and it was hardly his place to deny me an opportunity to enlighten the rest, so I ploughed ahead regardless.

'It seems extraordinary now, but the initial resistance to anaesthesia was immense. But no one could answer the argument that before performing the first recorded surgical operation, Our Lord cast Adam into a deep sleep.'

There was no reply.

'I am referring, of course, to the removal of a rib, in order to—'

'Yes, Professor Coote,' he cut across me. 'I know what you are referring to. I attended your classes.'

I heard his steps moving away from me, no doubt to fiddle with his tubes and valves, and I was left standing there, in open-mouthed awe of his rudeness.

That a snooze doctor quack should be so infernally arrogant to a Professor of Medicine almost beggared belief. This was a man whose profession consisted of squirting laughing gas in a person's face to knock them out. The process was only slightly more refined than it had been in the middle ages, when a patient would be made royally drunk, hit over the head or given mandrake root to induce oblivion. Even now he hardly had a pristine pedestal to stand on. Semi-poisoning patients with gas and oxygen is not yet an exact science, in either direction. I had witnessed a patient waking up during the amputation of his leg, and I would never forget it.

All the same, though, the ancients had a few tricks up their sleeves that can still make a curious modern surgeon, well, curious. The power of the mandrake root was believed in for such an immense span of time that one wonders why. I was particularly taken with the image of mandrake collectors of antiquity tying the plant to the collar of a dog and throwing a stick for the beast. All this so that they could cover their ears as the dog unwittingly pulled out the root. The shriek of an uprooted mandrake was meant to cause insanity or death.

Hundreds of years later Shakespeare said, through the luscious mouth of Cleopatra:

'Give me to drink Mandragora,

that I might sleep out this great gap of time
My Anthony is away.'

Turning from those beautiful, sonorous words, I
amused myself by imagining Moynihan on a com-
pulsory mandrake-gathering detail. Wearing his
only set of earmuffs, I stood watching him from a
rocky bluff, tickling the hairy tummy of his only
dog. Strange that in my fantasies I can always see.

The banging open of a door and a clatter of
metal instruments falling to the flags brought me
back to myself. Thinking back on it, what was most
arresting was the silence which followed. There was
no shout of annoyance or dressing down. There
was not even the scrape of the instruments being
retrieved; just a suspension of all activity.

'Sorry,' said the unmistakable voice of John
Geraghty. Still no one spoke. I wondered what on
earth they were all reading in his visage that
silenced them so.

When he spoke again, I thought that I could
hear it.

'She's ready,' he said.

Unbelievably, his voice was unsteady with emotion. I almost thought I could detect the welling of
tears behind those two words. I suddenly knew
that my initial impression the day of that first consultation had been right. Although it went against
all intuition, I understood now that John Geraghty
was in love with this disfigured child. I could
almost taste his passionate concern for her.

His fear that she would be snatched from him was no less than mine would have been if Alicia herself were lying outside, awaiting delivery to the attentions of Moynihan and Sweetman.

I acted instinctively, and, I still maintain, for the best.

'John,' I said. He did not reply, but I knew that he and all the room were listening, mindful of the seriousness of my tone.

'I would like you to deliver the anaesthetic.'

Both Sweetman and Moynihan spoke at once, but I interrupted them so quickly that I have no idea what exactly either of them had begun to say.

'She will have no idea who touches or cuts her once she is asleep, but while she is awake she should be handled only by familiar persons. John brought her to this. She trusts him.'

I heard footsteps striding towards the door and a flaccid slapping on the flags. By the time the door slammed, my mind had caught up with my ears: Moynihan had stormed out and had thrown his gloves to the floor.

I am not self-deluded. To evict the lumpen Moynihan *and* stamp my personality on the pro-ceedings gave me immense satisfaction, and my ego shouted out a childish 'Hurray!' My feeling at that moment could be neatly summed up by the country phrase: 'To kill two birds with one stone.'

'*Well*,' said Sweetman through audibly gritted teeth, 'since Mr Moynihan has understandably left

the theatre, we will have to accept this new arrangement. I presume you can vouch for Dr Geraghty's
competance?'

'I taught him,' I said simply.

'*Quite so*,' said Sweetman, malevolently.

The theatre was not silent now. The shift in
personnel brought with it a flurry of reorganisa-
tion. That fine actor, JJ Robinson, once described
to me the occasion of a performance of Richard
Brindsley Sheridan's *The Rivals* at the Abbey
Theatre. A relatively minor character was off sick,
although I believe the term 'sick' was a euphemism
for what the Dublin poor call 'mouldy'.

The company had a rolling understudy system,
by which every actor understudied every other. This
had the effect that when one player stepped into
the breach left by the absent drunk, it followed that
almost every other player was impersonating a character entirely new to them, each having to replace
the other. This presented a number of unforeseen
practical problems, and when one large actor
attempted to change into his third act costume, he
discovered that all the appropriately sized trousers
were already onstage.

The large actor in question was, of course,
Robinson himself. He made his entrance as Sir
Lucius O'Trigger with a floral tablecloth from the
green room draped about his loins. He looked like
a hottentot.

Moynihan's disappearance provoked a similarly

frantic redeployment, although I hoped not quite so makeshift. Amidst the bustle of rearrangement I could only wish that John would approach me. I wanted to have a quiet word with him, but I could not risk seeking him out. A stumbl, or worse, a fall, would undermine my precariously gained authority. I stood my ground, therefore, looking, I sincerely hoped, like an admiral gazing implacably out to sea at the start of some great campaign.

He approached me sure enough, but he didn't speak. There was no mistaking the smell of him, though. If he was habitually sour with sweat before, he must have been positively drenched in the stuff for the last few days. I had noticed it in Sweetman's office earlier, but close up the smell of him was overwhelming. Perhaps he would not have to anaesthetise the child at all; he could just lean over her.

'I take it that this will present no problems for you, John?' I said.

He seemed startled that I had detected him. Presumably he was not aware of his unusual personal must.

'Em ... no, no, not at all. I, er ... I ...' He stopped, something unspoken lingering in the air along with the stench.

'Yes?'

'You think it will reassure her?'

'Yes,' I said, truthfully, feeling no compunction to mention the additional benefit to me of infuriating both Moynihan and Sweetman. I allow myself these little peccadilloes by way of compensation for my blindness. I consider myself to have been extremely patient and accepting of my condition, and I reward myself by indulging in a little needling of irritating persons.

My words must have reassured John, for he moved away from me and in about five minutes the air around me was breatheable again.

I assumed that preparations, or rather reorganisations, were nearing completion, for a nurse approached me. I did not recognise her voice. I allowed her hands to gown and mask me and I felt a stab of humiliation when no gloves were proffered: my hands would not be in use.

It occurred to me to wonder who was with the child. Perhaps the country nurse who had touched my arm and spoken to me with respect; if so, I was glad. I had a vivid image of her in my mind for the first time that day, this child whose name I had internalised like a talisman.

In a moment of sentimentality, I pictured her small feet in white crocheted stockings beneath the covers, although of course she would be barefoot. Why I associate socks with vulnerability is anyone's guess. I did have a sock puppet snake when I was a child: Lord Hiss.

'Gentlemen ...' announced Sweetman, and I heard the theatre door swing open.

It had been five years since I had been present at an operation, yet the sounds as she came into the room were still so familiar that I felt I could see again. I could see the trolley coming through the door with its frail shape beneath the sheet; could see the spotless floor and the shining instruments lying on linen cloths on the wheeled table. All whiteness. White gowns and white masks, white caps as if all the persons present were Jews and Jewesses, I have often fancied.

Sweetman would be looking idiotic; his head wired up to an electric bulb, dangling just in front of his nose like an illuminated snot. Everyone would be anonymous and strange to the girl. Perhaps the smell of John Geraghty would be a comfort to her after all. It would at least be familiar.

He was speaking to her as the metal brakes snapped to on the trolley.

'. . . a mask over your mouth and one over your nose. It will smell a little rubbery, but the gas will make you go to sleep very, very quickly and . . .'

His voice was gentle and calm. None of the emotion I had detected earlier was apparent.

'. . . and then I will count backwards from ten, very slowly, and by the time I have reached five you will be asleep . . .'

I moved closer to his voice. He spoke to her continually as he applied the masks and adjusted the stopcocks and valves. It was strangely unsettling to overhear. His words seemed to me to be shockingly intimate, although they were not. Perhaps I had closed out the sounds of the room and was too close to him. I could smell him strongly again.

He told her that they were ready to begin, and I heard the slow hiss of the gas escaping from the cylinders ready to mix in the pipes that fed the masks. She had been silent all along. Now as the nitrous oxide mingled with the oxygen and touched her ravaged mouth, she made one single sound.

'*Ah!*'

A high, breathy sigh that in another context would have been sensual. Geraghty's voice was calm as he counted slowly backwards from ten.

Ten

I wish Kitty was here. Morrie left a note for her
when we got word for the hospital, but he left
Dolas in charge of it and I don't trust Dolas. My
bag had been sitting by the door for so long that
there was a film of dust on it when I picked it up.
That's another thing about Dolas. She never dusts
anything properly.

We went in the Edson – hurray! – for Kitty
always walks to mass, so we had our pick. She says
she can't be doing with the way everyone will stare
so at a woman driving a car to mass.

'Where does it mention motor cars in the Bible, would somebody mind telling me?' she said on her way out last Sunday, and Morrie looked over to me as if he couldn't believe his ears, because he'd only asked me the same thing two days ago.

'And Jesus came down in his Triumph!' he said, delightedly. 'I can't believe you fed me that!

Kitty just looked at him with one eyebrow half-way up her forehead and told him to stop buying the *Freeman's Journal*. She's very quick; that's exactly where he told me he got it.

I can't understand why she *ever* takes the motor car anywhere, because she is so full of life it would be terrible for her to die in a crash, and she always nearly crashes. She must be very lucky.

I am getting lucky too, for a wonder. I think that luck is the kind of thing that can rub off, so I'm glad that now I spend my time surrounded by lucky people like Morrie and Kitty, who are rich and love each other. Both of them are very good-looking too. They have what Cass calls 'on taw'. That is Gaelic for 'the luck.'

This room is very clean. Nurse Brigid tells me that's because of germs. The paint on the walls is shiny and green like the light-coloured mosses on Cass's slates. I imagine they have shiny paint so that they can just wipe it down. The floor is shiny tiles. It's as if the whole room was made especially so that you can clean it easily. I would like my kitchen to be shiny and easy to clean like this room.

I don't care for the pictures on the walls, though. They are quite alarming. People standing up with no hair on their heads and bits of their bodies opened out or peeled back to show the doctors how the land lies. I don't think they should have them in this room, for you don't like to think of a doctor having to belt out of the operation to check where some bit is; you'd really prefer them to know off by heart, but maybe doctors think such pictures are pretty decorations to be looking at. Make you wonder about marrying one.

I really wish there was something else to look at. One of them has no top to his skull, never mind hair, and his brain is sticking out of the top like a blackberry made of meat. Another one has no skin at all and he looks like someone mocked him up using just livers.

There is one very interesting one, though. He has all his skin and bits, and I imagine he must be just to show the spinster nurses, for he is fully equipped with everything a man could need. I must say I find that one very educational for there is detail on it that I wasn't aware of previously, and as Cass so rightly says, 'It's all grist to the mill.'

I can still smell him. He has a scent like no other person I have ever known. It stays in a room when he has left it and it was even stronger today, I noticed. I think his smell gets stronger the more he is around me, like a beast in heat. It makes me feel excited to think that I can make his smell stronger.

When he left just there, he gave me no idea of how long I would have to wait before they brought me inside into the theatre. I could not believe it when Brigid told me that where I would have my operation was called a theatre! I thought it was definitely a 'good omen', because one thing I have taken to most particularly lately is going to see plays or entertainments.

I even have a secret idea that I could be *in* a play when my face is fixed because it would be quite easy for me to say the words of the play passionately, what with all the build-up of silence in me. Another thing in my favour is that I have many years' previous experience of pretending things in my head, so I think I would be very well qualified. Also you can be on the stage *and* married so you could have your cake and eat it. And speaking of cake, the icing on it would be that I'm also extremely fond of dressing up, so I have everything going for me, really.

Brigid laughed at me when she saw my face and she said I wasn't to go expecting a curtain or anything. Actually she said the word 'anything' like this: 'enthin'. I like Brigid a lot, although she sounds very peculiar, like she's always chewing on a big wad of bread and she gurgles at the back of her mouth when she says ess. Another thing is that she has a very country way of speaking. But then she always did and she's no less nice for that.

I can't help thinking about the theatre, though. When I went to the Abbey with Morrie and Kitty,

I thought I had died and gone to heaven. It was a bit like being at mass except it was mostly not boring at all, God forgive me.

I thought the actors were quite good, although I am not without my own opinions on them. I felt they were foolish to impersonate country people in rags, living in a cottage not much better than Daddy's. When I am an actress I will definitely pretend to be a glamorous person with many suitors and fine clothes and intrigue. The words were invented by a man called Synge. The name suited him, for his words were so curious and his sentances so long that the actors and actresses sounded almost as if they were singing a song. If it had had less words and a nicer setting and clothes it would have been a good entertainment, in my opinion.

The actress who had most of the lines had two suitors and I felt that was a good part of it, although frankly, I thought she could have made more of the situation.

In all fairness, though, the suitors were not up to much, for one of them was a poor fish, flabby and mealy-mouthed, and the other bucko was not even able to kill his father, though he boasted that he had to puff himself up. Men can be terrible bags of air, I've noticed.

I suppose I can't give out too much about the actresses, for I am going to be in a theatre and I am dressed very poorly! I brought a nightgown that Kitty had bought for me, but when I got to the hospital they made me put on a gown that had hardly no back to it. It is plain at the front and I don't think it shows me off at all well, to say the least.

Dr Geraghty has been gone a long time now. I hope he is not too upset.

Brigid seems to be in a very funny mood and I don't mind admitting it's a little annoying. She keeps smiling at me and half laughing as if I was six years old and had done something charming. Just a minute ago she said this to me: 'You're a one!'

That doesn't seem to me to make any sense. You'd almost think she is a bit simple the way she's carrying on. She is kindly though.

I shouldn't say this, and I can hardly talk, I suppose, in my current situation, but I think Brigid is quite a plain woman. She has nothing wrong with her, needless to say, but the general effect is not of a raving beauty. She is big, for a start, which I think is never a good thing. Cass used to say a thing about certain ladies: 'Big-boned!'

And she let me know that that was a funny way of saying fat. Brigid is not fat exactly, but she is certainly big-boned. Her face is very nice and not like that creature who stole my brother, but it is nice in a way that a woman sees: kind and not at all haughty. A man would not like to look at Brigid for long, I think. I have come to believe that a man likes a woman to be a little bit cruel, but in a charming way.

Sometimes I think that I am in the best possible part of my life, for I am not yet finished; I have my beauty to come. It's like diving off a high, cold cliff and landing in a princess. Most women have what they have, and it is not always good enough to get them what they want; maybe that would be worse than being harelipped in this age of miracles.

Brigid keeps rubbing my hand and it is a very nice gesture to do, but it keeps distracting me from my thoughts and bringing me back into this shiny room. I wonder do they teach nurses to rub their patients' hands in nursing school. I bet they do and I imagine it is to calm a person down, but I want to be excited.

I feel like I have years of not being excited to make up for. Being nervous and mousey and obe-dient is not the same thing as being calm, although they are all the opposite of being excited. I never thought before that there can be two or three things the opposite of just the one thing. All my life before is the opposite of this moment.

This bed is on wheels. It is not really a bed at all, but more of a trolley. Mrs Scallon has just such a trolley, though smaller, which she calls a butler's tray although Kitty and Morrie don't have a butler. I'm like a pastry or a cake, sitting on a trolley wait-ing to be served up! I feel as rattly inside as teacups and spoons. If something doesn't happen soon I think my body will just rise off this bed and go sliding about on the shiny ceiling. I feel like I will scream.

Somebody just talked to Brigid through the door Dr Geraghty went in. I think they said the word 'Halpin.' I must be about to go in! I wish Kitty was here. Brigid is not going into the operation room, she said, and I don't know anyone else.

More men and women are going in. They are all wearing white and they have white cloths over their mouths. They are all harelipped maybe! Well, not really, my head is all over the place, I need to concentrate and not think mad things.

I am going in. The bed is moving and I am going through the door into the theatre. The light is so bright coming through the door that I can hardly see. The air is warmer in here, there are so many people, but I can smell his smell above all the rest of them.

It seems like everything is happening very fast now after all the waiting. There are people fiddling with my sheet and my gown and they are holding me down so that all I can see is the ceiling. There is a big electric light on the ceiling with a bulb in it that makes green light around everything I can see. I have turned away from it to look at a white person, but there is a horseshoe of green light right across the middle of his face. I don't know what is happening. But I don't need Kitty any more because I'm not afraid. All of those people are concentrating only on me, like I really am the star. I have never been so happy in my whole life.

He is speaking to me. I have closed my eyes and I will just listen to his voice and breathe him in. His smell is as familiar to me as my own smell. It is like burying my face into my armpit to see do I need a wash.

His face is close to me. His words are so near that I can hear when the spit in his mouth slaps off his teeth. I want him to speak more and calm me down, for my heart is leaping and I'm meant to be going off to sleep. I can smell rubber as the mask is lowered over my nose and mouth. It feels most peculiar.

He will count for me and I will sleep in ugliness and wake to beauty. He says, 'Ten,' and he says it calmly, but I can hear his need through the touch of his tongue off the roof of his mouth.

'Nine,' he says it cheerfully, disguising his emotion, but not from me.

'Eight,' I
'Seven,' am
'Six,' a
'Five.'

Eleven

They had put some kind of white cloth stuff over the mouth they had butchered. For some reason, that more than anything else choked me with rage and grief. Once her poor heart had stopped beating, they didn't even care enough to repair her dead face. They were going to send her to the grave more disfigured than she had come into the world.

It's strange the things that occur to you at moments like these, but as I looked at her, wearing that hateful gag, I saw her anew. O, Ellen, I thought, she looks just like you, your poor, ravaged daughter. A couple of inches of cloth was all it took to cover the ugliness beyond which none of us could see.

She was so young.

They had tied back her new bangs with a white Alice-band, and I could see that her brow was smooth and high like her mother's. Her open eyes were pale and sea-coloured, with lashes so fine they were frost-tipped almost. A square of fine net, almost invisible, covered her face against the flies; so vulnerable are the dead. She looked cold, as if she had frozen to death. What kind of creatures had left her eyes wide open? Isn't that what they do in books – gently reach out and close the eyes, before looking up and sorrowfully shaking their heads?

I once told Ellen she reminded me of the women in the Dutch paintings at the National Gallery in London and she laughed and cracked some joke that I don't remember any more, something rude about the Arnolfinis. Veronica, too, had those naked, timeless eyes, that bright forehead, and all any of us could ever see was her mouth.

I touched the blue and white ruffle of her favourite dress, and then I removed the 'modesty vest' of cloth that some prudish hand had placed over her white décolletage, and left her.

Dom, of course, was not there. He told Morrie that he had caught some wretched creature that doesn't normally grace our shores in his honey traps – once in a lifetime opportunity; an Arctic something – and he had found a buyer for it in Monastereven. Veronica, apparently, didn't rate high enough on his list of priorities to compete with the sale of a rare finch.

I'm sure Liam would have been there, but that imbecilic wife of his had poisoned the two of them on their honeymoon in Skerries by under-cooking cockles she bought from the side of the road. The woman hasn't the sense God gave a chicken and poor Liam was suffering for it, jostling her for prime position on the po, no doubt. His postcard to Veronica bravely attempted to make a joke of it, but his misery was so pathet-ically transparent that I couldn't bring myself to show it to her. Poor man can hardly write.

So it was up to Morrie and I to support our girl through her ordeal, which was just fine with us; we would have done anything for her.

Actually, for most of the morning it was up to Morrie alone. There was a note for me on the kitchen table when I came home from mass saying: 'All systems are go.' (Sometimes that man talks like he never left the army.) I didn't go into the kitchen until a quarter to one, however, because I was up at my writing desk getting through my correspon-dence as I *always* do on a Sunday and which he very well knows. If that man of mine wasn't practically an atheist, or if he ever *thought* for one second before doing things, I would have been there with him from the get go. As it was, he ended up taking on both the burden and the blame alone. It's just like him.

Neither Mrs Scallon nor Dolas managed to notice the foolscap-size note, with its urgent message written in block capitals and thrice underlined, sticking out of the toast rack and waving in the draught like a flag.

Goodness knows when I would have read the blessed thing if I hadn't suddenly had the most violent craving for an almond macaroon and a chat with my girl. I've always been fond of macaroons, especially since Mrs Scallon manages to float vanilla-flavoured air over rice paper and suspend a sliver of almond thereon. Delicious. However, ever since I started ballooning out with the Halpin heir, I have been consuming them in alarming quantities. I sometimes feel less like a pregnant woman than a glutton.

I spotted the note as soon as I entered the breakfast room, and immediately called Dolas's attention to it. She was actually wiping down the table when I came in, diligently cleaning *around* the toast rack, so she could hardly say she hadn't noticed the thing.

Her nose has been spectacularly out of joint since Veronica's arrival, so I wondered which of her annoying new defensive positions she would adopt: wheedling? sulking? ingratiating? affronted? It was all to play for.

Rather ingeniously, she went on the attack.

'Are you mad, Mrs Halpin?' she said, glaring at me. 'If I went around reading people's notes to other people I wouldn't last long in the one house, now would I?'

She nodded emphatically, in full agreement with herself. I swear that girl should be in the Dáil.

I pointed out to her that it would hardly be considered prying if she had merely shifted her carcass upstairs to tell me about the note's existence.

'I don't go around telling you how to be pregnant, do I?' she said, after regarding me for a moment with narrowed eyes. 'So I really don't think you should tell me how to do *my* job, Mrs Halpin.' And with that she *flounced* out the door, there really is no other word. I am certain she considered me comprehensively outfoxed.

There was hardly any point in taking two cars to the hospital, but I knew better than to enlist Mrs Scallon's help in engaging a taxi-cab. The woman is more pious than His Holiness, and she believes pregnancy to be a condition as shameful as syphilis. If she had her way I would have spent the last three months in a darkened room being spoon-fed beef tea and blancmange.

In fact, when Morrie and I finally plucked up the courage to tell her I was with child, he wrapped it up in so many euphemisms and delicacies, that at first she thought that we were asking her to make preparations for an unusually small house guest about whose gender we were unclear.

After a long, uncomfortable silence she turned to me and said quietly, 'Are they with the circus, Mrs Halpin?' and I had to explain it in less delicate language. The woman turned the colour of the bedlinen she was carrying in her arms, and my husband shook silently beside me, tears running down his face.

Morrie was sitting on a wooden bench in a corridor when I got to Sir Pat's. Something about the sight of him sitting there all alone raised a tenderness for him in me. Men always look so very vulnerable when they're idle, I always think.

Once, when I was walking home from school in the rain, I chanced upon my father waiting for an omnibus with a dripping newspaper over his head, clutching a soggy paper bag. I felt so sorry for him that I started to cry.

The fact that the paper bag turned out to contain a tin of highly contraband Yang-tse opium, and he was waiting for the bus because he had smashed the brougham and two into a tree, has in no way diminished the poignancy of this memory. Ellen always said I was soft as a marshmallow's mattress.

However, on this occasion I don't believe I was being sentimental. Even the best and most capable of people seem like bewildered children in a hospital. It's simply a fact that people just like us die and are cured within these strange-smelling walls every day, and the sobering truth is that we haven't the slightest notion how it is done. They are magicians and we are all frightened white rabbits cowering in the false bottom of the hat.

Morrie looked relieved to see me, although he questioned my late arrival with a quizzical tilt of his head. Luckily for him I was still feeling quite sentimental, so I contented myself with saying, 'Don't ask. Though, needless to say, it's your own fault.'

'O,' said Morrie.

A nurse clopped down the corridor carrying an enamel basin. Morrie and I watched her pass us like urchins gawking at a duchess. She did not even glance at us, but marched grimly on as if we were not there. There is a sniff of the past about our modern hospitals with everyone garbed in white like Dutch nuns. I suppose it's to place them above the vagaries of mere fashion, and connect them with a more austere and serious age. Personally, however, it gave me the shivers. The thought of submitting to their chilly care within the next few months made me most uncomfortable.

'Don't let them intimidate you, Kit,' said my husband, grinning. 'Just imagine what's going to be in that basin the next time she has to pick it up.'

I wish I could say that I had some presentiment of tragedy as I sat there waiting for Veronica to emerge, but the truth of it is that I was not really thinking about her at all. I was so proud of Morrie and I for getting her to this point that I was basking in self-satisfaction.

I fully believed that after losing Ellen, I had endured my allotted penance in this life. I was naïve. The pain of her death had eventually been replaced by a kind of insane self-confidence. Although I could never have articulated it, I believed that the world could no longer hurt me and therefore my actions could never again have negative consequences. I thought it was my own strength of character that made the world so pleasant for me to inhabit. What a child – what children we both were. We were bullet-proof.

Now, my naïveté seems incomprehensible, but you see, my life divides through a precise point that contains the fact of Veronica's death. A time when events were understandable, and a time directed by caprice.

'What exactly are we waiting for, Morrie?' I suddenly thought to ask. We are such sheep really. The weightiness of the hospital and the sight of my husband sitting still for a change had driven that logical question from my mind. I realised that I didn't know what stage in the procedure we had reached.

'They're making her ready,' he said. 'Didn't I tell you?'

'No. You didn't.'

He took my hand in his, and I felt the clamminess of it. I resisted the urge to wipe it on my coat, for a man doesn't really understand the nature of a wife's peculiarities when she is expecting.

I smiled at him. He looked, to use my mother's word, discombobulated. I will never get used to seeing men out of their sphere of influence. I find it unbearably poignant.

I was relieved at the distraction of footsteps coming down the corridor towards us, for waiting for anything at all is terribly boring, I find. A nurse was clearly approaching Morrie and I, for she was smiling and nodding as she walked. Her unsettling white garb was touchingly streaked at the breast pocket, where she had failed three times to house her pen.

'Mr and Mrs Halpin?' she asked brightly, with one of those comical lisps that click and whistle over the back teeth on the letter 's'.

Knowing my husband as I do, I nodded vigorously and squeezed his hand tightly to stop us both from laughing. Unfortunately, his palm was so sweaty that squeezing it made it shoot out from my grasp like a rifle loaded with an eel. As you can imagine, this did nothing to sober our mood. We have always been terrible at setting each other off, particularly in tense situations, funerals and the like.

I covered my mouth and Morrie put his arm around me and buried his face in my shoulder. At this point, I did a disgraceful thing and tried to pretend that I was upset. The friendly nurse looked at us both with absolute bewilderment, visibly racking her brains for the cause of our sudden breakdown.

Morrie and I were taking deep breaths, and just about getting back to ourselves, when she spoke again. 'She'll be fine! Sure don't fret yee'rselves.'

A sentence that contained so many 's's set us off again. I felt just awful – she seemed so perfectly lovely – but it was very hard to regain control. To my surprise, Morrie managed it first.

'Forgive us, nurse,' he said in a strained voice, compassion fighting against hysteria. 'My wife, as you can see, is expecting and she gets quite emotional at times. And, er ... I get upset when she does.'

We both looked up at her at this point, genuine tears in both our eyes. She looked back at us as if we were insane, but she was not the kind of person to be unduly disturbed by insanity.

'Fair enough, so,' she said. 'Just to tell you that she's gone into theatre, and I'll let you know when you can see her.'

'Thank you, nurse,' said Morrie weakly, in the chastened tone of a recalcitrant schoolboy.

'Mr Sweetman says you may wait in his rooms, and I'll bring you some tea. Will you follow me?' And off she went, a reassuring picture of normality in sensible shoes.

We trotted after her down a bewildering labyrinth of corridors. I really felt as if we should have been dropping breadcrumbs behind us, in case the nurse turned out to be evil and abandoned us in the deepest thickets of Sir Patrick Dun's.

Eventually, we turned into a wider, brighter corridor: a bright demesne in the centre of poor hamlets. The doors on this corridor were dark panelled wood, and twice the width of the doors in the rest of the hospital. She showed us in.

'I'll bring ye some tea,' she said, and disappeared, presumably relieved to get shut of us.

Morrie and I looked at each other, grinning, and I don't mind admitting that he crossed the room to me and kissed me most affectionately.

'Rogue,' he said.

'Sweaty-palmed rogue!' I replied.

We were happy, you see.

The room was elegant and ordered. A truly enormous desk with papers laid on it with geometric precision dominated the room. Hundreds of tomes lined the shelves, arranged in height order, which made me instantly take a 'set' against the occupant. Books are for grabbing from a shelf in a moment of impulsive inquiry, or discovering under a bed like a cheeky old friend.

'I'd say he's a bit po-faced, is he?' I asked.

'Bang on. But a damned good surgeon everybody says. Precise.'

'Let's never have him round to dinner then, agreed?'

'He'll never darken our door,' replied Morrie, settling into Sweetman's chair. He brought his hands together and placed them under his chin and said, in a ponderous voice, 'And tell me, Mrs

Halpin: are you quite sure the child you are carrying is your husbands'?'

I squealed with laughter and rushed around to take the patient's chair and act outraged. When I sat into it, however, I found myself being catapulted backwards, before being bucked forward and practically deposited onto the table.

'Dear Christ!' said Morrie, racing round to help me up. 'What kind of a lethal contraption is that?'

Once I had struggled to my feet, feeling most undignified, we made an examination of the offending piece of furniture. Lower than you ever beheld, the blessed chair was on springs! The man had a sprung chair for sick people to sit down on unawares. I had said it before and I said it now: 'Surgeons are evil.'

'A necessary evil, I grant you,' Morrie conceded.

He looked at my disheveled appearance and smiled. 'You should have seen yourself!'

I looked around the room for a mirror, feeling instinctively that Sweetman would have at least one. He did. I was rearranging my clothes in front of it when the nurse came back in. She was not carrying a tray.

She stood in the doorway without speaking for a moment, staring from one of us to the other without blinking her eyes. She looked frozen.

I think in my heart of hearts I knew then, but the shock of seeing her frightened face stopped all conscious thought. I could not look away from her even as far as Morrie. It seemed as though time had stopped.

'Mr Halpin,' she said eventually. 'Professor Coote needs to speak to you immediately.'

I did not find her voice amusing now: I found it chilling. To hear a cheerful person deliberately emptying their voice of emotion tells you as much as the emotion they fear to betray.

'What has happened?' Morrie's voice was barely audible, and I looked over to him and saw that he was looking at the floor. I found that I could not look at her either, as if the impact of what she might say could be lessened somehow by not seeing her face.

'Professor Coote would like to speak to you himself, Mr Halpin,' she said in that terrible, mechanical voice. 'I'll get some tea for you, Mrs Halpin.'

And she opened the door and stepped over the threshold and stopped there, waiting.

Morrie turned to me, his eyes already glistening, but neither of us could think of what to say. Strangely, I don't think either of us considered any possibility other than that Veronica was dead, so what was there to say?

I don't know why I let Morrie be led away from me by that nurse. I should have insisted on going with him, but I accepted her command like a sheep.

Waiting alone in that sterile room, I began to hear the tick of Sweetman's clock for the first time, although it must have been there all along. I waited in a kind of suspended state, thinking not about Veronica, because I could not, but about the dank smell of Sweetman in the room. His fastidiousness obviously did not extend to his person.

The hard winter light through the window made my eyes water. Strange that the light should do that and not Veronica. You see, at that time I had not yet seen her face.

Twelve

Sweetman had dismissed the last of his team, and we were alone with the poor child. She had breathed her last not three minutes ago, and I suspected his haste in clearing the room to have a purpose.

The change in her had been sudden and brutal.

Sweetman had just made the primary incisions along the free margins of the cleft. I know this because he narrated his actions for the benefit of his junior staff. I'm sure describing the scene for me was merely an unavoidable side effect.

Without warning, there came a bucking and convulsing from the table. I instinctively moved forward, and then bethought me and stepped back, to let them help her. I'm sure they were perfectly efficient, but the sounds gave the impression of panic and confusion. Metal instruments fell to the floor as they tried to restrain and assist her, and as the trolley began to rock and shudder under her convulsing body, I heard a table of equipment overturn. Someone ran from the room, crashing through the double doors, no doubt to replace a damaged instrument, although it sounded like flight.

It was my first time to hear a death and not to see it, and it was unsettling. Of course I knew what was happening. The child was undergoing a massive seizure. It happens, and I could not lay any blame at Sweetman's door, deliciously tempting though that would be.

At such an early stage in a procedure it was much more likely to have been a reaction to the anaesthesia, an allergy or intolerance. Such things are precisely the kind of ill-chances against which a relative signs away the hospital's liability. A malevolent traitor in the body, undetected, meets a colourless gas that is harmless to thousands, and Veronica Broderick bucks and gags on the trolley, as if the vital spark were being exorcised.

There was one other possibility. I fervently hoped that no blame attached itself to John Geraghty. It is possible that a misdelivery of the anaesthetic could have caused her to seizure, but I found that immensely difficult to accept, for a number of reasons.

Firstly, if the patient had no constitutional vulnerability in that regard, the anaesthetist would have to deviate significantly from the norm to cause such a devastating effect. It is the kind of thing one might fear, for example if the man were drunk or incapacitated in some way. Geraghty was simply too good a practitioner to fail like that.

And then there was the second consideration. If I was right, he was in love with the child or at least passionately concerned for her, of that much at least I was certain. It would be hard to explain in a court of law, but I heard his tenderness towards her, and it moved even a hardened old bugger like me. Whatever else, he would not have been careless.

I was ninety-nine per cent confident in my mind of what had happened. The lingering percentage point was merely an unyielding guilty conscience around the dismissal of Moynihan: I would find it hard to sleep that night if I had delivered her to her fate.

I could feel my inner Alicia noting the turmoil I had caused in the theatre just before the surgery, quite deliberately and – I admit it – with no little enjoyment. One's inner Alicia is in possession of far more ammunition than the real thing. She can ask the questions that the rational inner Coote would dismiss as poppycock. Had I created a tension that caused mistakes to be made? My instinct as a surgeon was that I had not, but as a man I had my doubts. One lingering percentage point of them.

Sweetman and I stood in silence. I felt less antagonism towards him now. In fact, I felt a kind of pity. Losing a patient on the table is awful, no matter what your level of experience, all the more so when the patient is a child.

'We need a post-mortem,' said Sweetman. He sounded exhausted. 'You might talk to the family?'

'I imagine they'll balk at it,' I replied, the memory of Morrie's squeamishness vivid in my mind. I remember clearing phlegm from his father's rotten lungs to help the poor man breathe. Morrie threw up so violently he had to be admitted, and rarely visited his father thereafter.

However, on this occasion I agreed with Reggie Sweetman. We needed a post-mortem.

Even in my own circle, the story of our little Cinderella had touched many people. Very few people had actually met her, for she was understandably shy of her appearance, so she could be mythologised by those who had not seen her into some pretty maiden with just a whisper of a scar, marring her otherwise perfect beauty, instead of the terribly disfigured unfortunate she actually was.

She had attained a kind of celebrity, this strange little waif. Her latest charming antics spread around the town as anecdotes. Every naïve misunderstanding and feral faux pas was broadcast by the gossips as if it concerned their own child or grandchild. The little nobody's child had become like the heroine of a magazine's serial story, which was just coming to its exciting climax.

This unfortunate ending would need some kind of explanation to pour cold water on the rumours that would inevitably be circulated by those who missed their fix of drama. God knows, they would probably have her murdered in cold blood by a jealous society beauty disguised as a nurse unless we provided something mundane and preferably in Latin.

Besides, I wanted to know.

It occurred to me that I might use Morrie's over-sensitivity to our own advantage.

'Cover her mouth and send him down here,' I said. I was willing to bet that Morrie would agree to anything in order to avoid sharing a room with a dead body.

'Really?' said Sweetman, doubtfully.

'Trust me,' I said. 'Just make sure his wife stays put, will you?' I added. I had no intention of including the scintillating Kitty. She had too much of the 'Alicia' about her; nothing got past her.

Sweetman tended to the child for a moment, and went to leave, but then stopped abruptly and turned back to me.

'By the way,' he said casually. 'Just so you know, whatever the result of that post-mortem, I will always hold you responsible for that child's death, *always*. Because even if it wasn't your foul-smelling little acolyte's direct malpractice that killed her, you compromised her care at the last minute, just to be the centre of attention. When you go to sleep tonight, ask yourself if Moynihan, with his twelve years of experience exclusively in anaesthesia, mightn't have picked up something early enough to save her that your locum missed. Even blind, you're dangerous.' And with that he left.

His vehemence shocked me, and, if the truth be told, his words went deeper than they should have. I suppose I had been accusing myself in the same vein, and hearing that accusation in another's mouth sent a jolt of guilt through me. I think that is what unsettled me, along with the helplessness of hearing someone die and being able to do nothing to help. Whatever the cause, I started to have the oddest sensations.

The room itself had a curious acoustic, and as Reggie Sweetman's furious steps receded, a silence swelled to fill the void, like a symphony. The walls resounded with nothingness. I stood transfixed as the ghostly emptiness played on my senses. And then I heard something that made my heart stop for a beat: a sound.

It was a simple, rhythmical noise that I should have been able to decode, but, maddeningly, it eluded my understanding. The sound toyed with me for what seemed an age, and then the hairs on my neck recognised it and stood up in horror. Something liquid was dripping from the trolley to the floor. The sound was obscenely loud and musical, almost beautiful. It was her blood.

I have no explanation for what happened next, I can only record my experience honestly and accurately. Suffice it to say, it was against character. I was not myself for the next ten minutes.

As the blood dripped to the floor, it made my body shiver under my clothes. My sweat had cooled there and all of a sudden I was frozen with it. My body tensed as if against some nameless dread and I was literally paralysed with fear. I struggled against the rising panic I was feeling, but found that I could not move.

Into my mind, unbidden, came a thought, and I am incredulous now that I could *ever* have formed such a thought, so transparently did it declare its opposite: 'I have no fear of the dead.'

This ludicrous, womanish thought persisted; it was all I could think. Although I knew it to be a superstitious, shamanistic notion, and searched my mind for a rational antidote, I found my lips mouthing it again, at the very edge of utterance.

'I have no fear of the dead.'

Still I could not move, but stood frozen as adrenaline dripped onto my heart, preparing me for action that would not come. This dead child did not frighten me, *could* not.

No. It was the sound of her blood relentlessly hitting the floor that terrified me. The horror I felt was without content. It was animal.

I searched my mind for physic, like a man rifling frantically through a cabinet.

'I am a professor of medicine,' I thought. That was good.

'This is an attack of anxiety, nothing more.' Better. I felt a tiny freeing-up inside me, an inch of latitude on either side of the fear. I groped about for a thought or a memory that would calm me, actively seeking remedy.

As naturally as sunshine breaking through a cloud, my mind came to rest in the quiet front room of my childhood home. It was so real that I could see again the dresser, heavy with lilies, smell their languorous scent on the dusty air.

I was eight years old once more. I turned from the flowers to gaze tenderly on my dead father's face. They could not keep me away from his open coffin those three long days of his lying out. I would out-stay my mother and brothers and then, in secret, I would touch his yellow face, cold and familiar like my bedside candle.

His presence was sternly companionable and I felt emboldened to speak to him under my breath. I had him to myself now, formally offering him chatty parcels of information, as if I was writing him a letter.

I described his own appearance to him, as a courtesy, since he could no longer see it. But I was careful to couch it in complimentary language, dwelling on how dignified and fine he looked.

Occasionally, the smell of the undertaker's preservatives troubled my senses, elusive as the scent of violets, but I never mentioned it to him for fear of embarassing him.

I felt very grown up, knowing exactly what to do and say, for I could not really be wrong. It was not like being with another person exactly; not so difficult.

Alone in the deserted theatre, beside the dripping corpse of a child, I felt the memory of my long-dead father bring me back to life. He drew me forth, comforted his terrified son: a sixty-seven-year-old professor of medicine.

Then I did something that I have for years ridiculed in others. A pet hate if you will.

I joined the ranks of the cat-chatters, the plant whisperers, the ones who spill their guts to gravestones: those who cannot be alone. For the first time since my father's death six decades ago, I talked to one who could not hear or understand me.

'Well, Veronica,' I said, turning my head towards her corpse, unmanning myself. 'You're quite a little witch, aren't you?'

Only her dripping blood answered me.

It was at that precise moment that I suddenly realised what, exactly, I was hearing. I realised the insanity of fearing the sound of her blood, rather than asking the blindingly obvious question: *Why the hell had she bled so much?*

I stepped carefully towards the trolley, and felt the slick under my shoes. The floor was thick with it. My heart was pounding as I tried to think back to just before her fatal seizure.

I had been distracted, to be sure; preoccupied with a fear of knocking something over or jogging an elbow. It was not the fatherly presiding-over I had envisaged. I was frustrated, feeling left out. All that, certainly. But I had listened.

After his initial incisions, Sweetman had announced his intention to extend anteriorly from the apex of the cleft. *But he had not done so.* Just as he had said the words, the first seizure took her. Indeed, now that I was thinking clearly, at no point in the procedure should she have been capable of producing a torrent of blood that spills over and hits a polished floor like drumming rain. Her only wounds should have been minor, even if she had shaken free the clamps during her fit. Something was dreadfully amiss.

No wonder the blood disturbed me so. My rational mind, in possession of information that my eyes could not help to process, was telling me that something was very wrong. What I had been told did not match what my senses were telling me.

My mind was racing now. Christ! I could do with a stiff drink. How long had I stood after Sweetman left? Minutes. Yes, several minutes at least before I heard the blood. It followed then that Sweetman had not seen it. Couldn't have!

Otherwise he would never have agreed to bring Morrie to the place. If that was the case, how the hell could he have missed it?

There was no doubt in my mind that the child had had a massive seizure. I had heard it myself, the sounds were unmistakable. And there was no doubt that she had died. But there was something terribly strange about this death.

I inched over to the trolley, feeling a rush of excitement. The floor was wet where I was standing. I reached out my hands and found a limb, felt her cooling flesh under the thin gown. A leg. I let my hands rove upwards, searching, half turning her to locate the hidden wound. I could feel no dampness in the gown above, no trickles except around her opened mouth, where one clamp still remained under the cloth that Sweetman had placed over it.

And then, I heard it, over to my left, beyond where I stood fumbling at the flesh of this dead child.

The slosh of a sink full to overflowing. I heard the slap of water hitting the floor like a waterfall of coins at an amusement arcade, dislodged by a single ha'penny: a dripping tap left running indifferently by a preoccupied medical team.

My hands recoiled from her as if I had touched a live cable. I felt that I had violated her with my deluded examination; the profundity of my guilt was now exposed to me.

She was my own tell-tale heart.

I stood in the empty theatre and I laughed a short, bitter laugh at myself. There was no mystery about her death, no blood-lusting stranger who had sought her end. No indeed. Only persons here present: dead girl and old, blind vain man. A man who wanted to be important once again and was content to locate his conscience in his wife – outside of himself where he need not heed it. Cock-fool man!

'I answer to that description.'

Beatrice, *Much Ado about Nothing*. Funny that! Much ado about nothing: that would neatly summarise my attitude to Alicia's infernal harping on about the child's father – his name, his bloody name!

I did know the man's name. He was Dominick Broderick, and it was I who had persuaded Morrie Halpin to bypass his consent and sign himself her next of kin. At my behest he was told nothing about the surgery we would perform on his child. The reason? O, very simple. I did not wish his consent to be sought because I was sure he would not give it.

Geraghty told me he was afraid for her.

I have been fearless in many aspects of my life. I have allowed little to stand in my way, and I have achieved much through bloody-minded determination. For that reason, I didn't hesitate for a moment to do what I suddenly realised was necessary. You would think that such a profound revelation of fault would have engendered in me a desire for one heroic act of reparation. Not so, indeed.

As I coldly looked upon the man that I was, I resolved to act according to my lights. There would be no post-mortem, no opportunity for recriminations: no scenes. Sure and for damn no apologies! I would sign the death certificate and then I would concentrate all my considerable talents on forgetting.

The swing doors opened and a woman's voice said, 'Professor Coote.' Despite the gravity of the moment, I found the voice comical; speech impediments piled one atop the other, even on those two words.

'I've brought . . .' she broke off. She must have seen the child.

'O!' she said, and sobbed into her hand, each wet sound like the beginning of some anguished word. I was shocked at her emotion, and worried in case something I had done had made the scene more distressing than it already was, but she allayed my fears.

'I'm sorry, sir,' she said, composing herself a little. 'I've been with her all morning, and it's a shock to see her. I knew her from home, poor creature. I have Mr Halpin waiting outside.'

Delighted to have such an unexpected ally, I ordered her to mop up the damned water and to quickly arrange the child's body: 'To make it less distressing for Mr Halpin.'

When she finished, I decided to make further use of her.

'As soon as I have finished talking to Mr Halpin, have her laid out.'

'Yes, sir,' she said softly, and she turned to leave. I was so pathetically grateful that she did not challenge my authority that I almost cried. I felt a surge of warmth towards her, and as the swing doors swung to I called out to her: 'Do it yourself, would you? I think you were fond of her?'

'Yes, sir,' she said, and there was a smile in her voice. Rather touchingly, she added, 'She told me the frock she had on this morning was her favourite.'

'Then that is what she shall wear,' I said in an avuncular tone. 'Thank you, nurse. You can send Mr Halpin in now.'

Unspoken, of course, was that she would be dressed for the grave, and not stripped for a post-mortem examination. I sensed that it would not be difficult to dissuade anyone from subjecting the poor child's body to any further indignities. The image of those infernal white, crocheted stockings came into my mind, like the frontispiece of a novel. Little L-shaped silos of sentimentality!

A truly balanced and effective man can take his happiness wherever he finds it. I hope it will not seem insensitive when I confess that by the time the funny-voiced nurse had left to fetch poor Morrie, I was beginning to rather enjoy myself.

Thirteen

A beggar child scampered after us as we climbed the filthy steps of Harcourt Street Station, proffering a primrose rosette, roots and all. It was perfectly fresh, so she had, no doubt, uprooted it from Stephen's Green or somewhere close by. I don't usually deal in stolen goods, but something in her expression touched me and I nodded to Morrie to give her a coin. The transaction completed, she disappeared at a run, no doubt to uproot another flower, brave enough to withstand the February cold.

The station was terribly unkempt, as I had pointed out at length to the station-master when we travelled down to poor Liam's wedding. It seemed incredible that we should be making the journey again only three days later, and alone. Veronica had been in a sombre mood that day, but she still displayed her natural curiosity, fingering the chipped automatic machines and perusing the layers and layers of torn advertisements that lined the walls. At one point she tugged on my sleeve and brought me to show me one of them that had taken her fancy.

'Liverpool Virus Rat and Mouse Poison: THEY DIE OUTSIDE!'

I can see her now, her veiled head lowered, smiling behind the hand that covered her mouth, eyes glinting with amusement.

While Morrie and I sat in the grimy waiting room, she lingered among the stand of milk cans, looking about her with eyes that missed nothing. She seemed always to graduate to simple things, practical things. So much of her time was spent in the kitchen with Mrs Scallon and 'dreary Dolas' (Morrie's expression, I hasten to add) that I often felt quite jealous. It was quite a joke amongst us.

I suppose the poor creature had cooked and scrubbed for so much of her life that she could not be idle. Because she could not speak, I felt uneasy calling her to my room unless there was some 'thing' that could be the focus of our attentions. I was afraid our time together might somehow fall flat, that I might display an awareness of her disfigurement. I always looked at her eyes, flicking from one to the other, desperate not to stare at her mouth. I would not for the world have made her feel less than beautiful.

I suppose that is why I spoiled her. If I felt lonely, I'm not proud to admit that I would make the short walk to Grafton Street to find some pretty thing for her, a hat or a ribbon or at one point a set of combinations! These I would use as an excuse to lure her upstairs and revel in her innocent enjoyment. Her delight was really breathtaking, her whole skin seemed to illuminate from within, like one of those insects that glow in the dark.

Morrie purchased the tickets and I stared at the serried ranks of milk cans, awaiting dispatch, and marvelled that they should still be here and she gone.

We really should have travelled down yesterday, but truly, we were not in any condition to do so. Morrie was so shaken and terribly grief-stricken that I insisted he should not drive, particularly as there was talk of a great freeze. That *I* should not drive was taken as read.

I was not much better myself, if the truth be known, and when I remembered that Dom had travelled to Monasterevin, I reasoned that he might well not return till morning. Morrie said nothing to argue with me, so we stayed put.

In hindsight, we probably should have got it over with, for last night was fearful. I lay awake, thinking of her. I would see her dressing up, posing and coyly looking at me with her shy, lowered face. And then, inevitably, I would see her dead face again, at once vulnerable and implacable, the light behind her skin snuffed out. Such images played in my mind like a disturbing motion picture, the night through.

And occasionally, which frightened me the most, I would see Dom's face. Not as I saw him last, wary and truculent, accepting a gift for one of the children, but happy and proud to bursting as he walked down the aisle clutching the arm of his radiant Ellen.

I think I was afraid to sleep, because I didn't want the morning to come. Several times I looked across to Morrie and each time his eyes were wide open too, but for once I could not speak to him or share my misery.

It was six o'clock in the morning when Dolas knocked on the door of the bedroom to inform us that the Edson had been 'borrowed', as the current phrase goes. I think it showed a certain sensitivity on her part that she did not appear to be actually gloating, as she would normally do. In fact, she had been kindly to Morrie and I since we got back from Sir Patrick Dun's with the terrible news.

Unlike everyone else we know, Morrie had chosen to keep the car unlocked in compliance with another insane law from our esteemed government. Not only had they been happy to tear the country apart to gain office, they then proceeded to turn kindergarten teacher, crippling the law-abiding citizen with a series of ever more petty laws, the latest of which was that one could not lock one's car 'in case a policeman needed to move it' – this in a city that even the police are calling 'little Chicago'.

The lines started to hum, and we stepped out of the waiting room onto the platform to await the train. There were not many people on the platform at this early hour. Tired men in suits and hats, probably on their way to work in provincial banks and offices, and young domestics, shivering in cheap coats or pulling threadbare fox-furs tighter around their shoulders. On another occasion I would be thanking God for my great good fortune, but today I would willingly have swapped places with any of them.

The train arrived, absurdly loud, and we boarded. We found seats easily and I sat facing my husband, still too numb to talk to him. Through the window the train began to greedily devour the fourteen miles to Shannack. The pistons thrust hypnotically, lulling my senses, and, inevitably I suppose, my mind wandered back to the first time I made the journey, twenty years ago. Our mother's sister Ada had invited us to stay with her for the summer holidays. Ellen was seventeen, and I was twelve.

She seemed so grown-up to me, in her long travelling coat and her soft hair piled up on her head. Although I loved her to distraction, I was hopelessly jealous of her as I sat in my short dress and dangled my feet just above the floor. In my mind she is always the grown-up, though now I am older than she will ever be. Perhaps it is because I remember her in the fashions of another age.

The train bumped over something on the line, and my head knocked against the window. Nostalgia was threatening to overwhelm me, so I turned my mind to present matters.

'You don't suppose he may come up to the hospital to see her after all and we'll cross with him? I mean, he can't have no concern for what happens to her, can he?'

Morrie just looked at me. His eyes seemed sore with tiredness, and there was a look in them that disturbed me. I know when he is holding back.

'What?' I said, and did not shift my gaze. Still he said nothing.

'*What?*' I said again when he did not answer me. Then I recognised the look in his eyes. A weak, guilty look that I have always detested in him. I could hardly believe it.

'*You didn't tell him it was yesterday, did you?*' I said in horror, knowing before he slowly nodded that it was true.

Morrie's eyes filled up, but I had no pity for him. I think I loathed him in that instant.

'I was afraid he would change his mind, Kit,' he said. 'Think about it! If nothing had gone wrong it would have been the very best way!' He spoke in a shouted whisper now, hunching his head in an attempt to be simultaneously forceful and surreptitious.

'You know how he is! He's bloody-minded and he hates us. I think he kept her from that operation all those years half to spite me!' he went on, desperately trying to justify himself to me, or more probably, to himself. People were beginning to turn towards us and stare.

'No, Kit, I really do! Edward's advice was bang on. Just imagine how upset she would have been if he had come up and refused to give his consent.'

He stopped and lowered his eyes again, transparent as a window, and furious with himself for giving himself away.

'*Who consented to the operation?*' I said under my breath, turning away from him. I could not look on his face.

Morrie said nothing for a moment, and then in an even voice he said, 'I did. I told them that her father did not care about her. I told them that he had washed his hands of her because she was disfigured, and that I was her next of kin. They took my word, of course. I'm rich.'

'And *Monasterevin*? The Arctic whatsit?' I asked, still facing away from him.

'O, Kit,' he said quietly after a moment.

We spoke no more for the rest of the journey. For some reason, the calculation behind my husband's invented rare bird tipped the balance of my outrage to absolute. But it's strange, after a moment it was as if I had completely forgotten about him, as if he were an irrelevancy. I had shut him out.

An odd calm came over me and I ran my hand over my belly, idly looking out the window. Condensation was loosening into drops and the grey sky reflected through them, splitting the light and making a thousand landscapes. It was bizarrely beautiful. The panic of the morning receded, and my heart turned, undistracted, towards the man whose child we had stolen. I was overwhelmed with pity: we might as well have sent him a ransom note.

I have spent so much of my life hating Dominick Broderick that a moment's pity for him shook my understanding of the past like a kaleido-scope.

She met him that very summer, 1910, in the woods of Aunt Ada's estate. He was poaching. I never knew what passed between them as she never told me. It was the only area of her life that she would not share with me and I suppose some part of me never forgave her for excluding me. After her death, when I was a grown woman, I wondered if perhaps she was reticent because of my age; that Dom Broderick's fascination for her was sexual, animal. Certainly, he kept her almost continually pregnant, even if she could not keep most of them alive inside her.

Only once that summer did she mention him. We were getting ready for bed, saying our prayers kneeling beside Ada's high brass bedsteads with the green candlewick covers. The last of the evening's light glowed orange through her hair as she knelt there, muttering something vehemently. And when we had blessed ourselves she looked up at me. She wore an expression I had never seen before; if she had not been smiling I would have said she was incandescent with rage. I suppose it was passion.

'*I've found him!*' she said, hungrily. But no matter how much I tickled and badgered and poked her, she would say no more. I suppose it's no wonder I hated him.

Their courtship was certainly efficient, I'll say that for him. Within eight months they were married, my parents' hearts were broken and Ellen began the first of her seven pregnancies, the last of which would kill her.

It's strange, but no one meeting Dom Broderick without her could possibly imagine how much *fun* Ellen was; how droll and unpredictable. Ellen always said that we intimidated him and that we never got to see the Dom that she adored. She used that word about her husband: adored.

When Veronica was born five pregnancies after Liam, we went to visit her, bringing flowers and expensive baby clothes. She held her towards me, with a radiant look only slightly dimmed by tiredness and said, 'Isn't she *beautiful*?' There was no trace of irony or defiance. To Ellen, Veronica was beautiful just as she was.

The train started to slow, and I realised that my eyes were soft with tears. Something hard had broken inside me, a hatred, I suppose. What rotten timing it has all been, I thought as the train juddered to a stop. I glanced over at Morrie, who was still looking at me like a kicked dog. But I had no approval for him. I hadn't much for myself.

He walked behind me in silence, that husband of mine, as we approached the cottage along the boreen. There was no beauty in this backwater, only nominally a part of the Shannack townland. I felt abnormally alive to everything as I walked along the track, taking in each rusted byre and makeshift fence. Only a fool would believe the current wisdom, that all that is of the country is somehow innocent and spiritual. In this scrubby place, the wildness had been encroached upon just enough to ruin it and not sufficiently to make it civilised. It was a half place. A nowhere.

Since I had no wish to get to where I was going and no joy in my companion, I dawdled, dragging my feet through the muck like a child. Everywhere there was dung. Horse dung and cow dung and the pellets of some smaller creature that a city girl like me couldn't recognise. A sheet of old newspaper, battened down by the wind, moulded itself to a hedgerow and a dead fox, divided through the middle by the track of a tyre, decorated the road. What a place to grow in.

I slowed even more as the cottage came into view. Large, unruly dark hedges shaded it from the sunlight and a small carcass lay on the path to the door, picked clean. I had always thought the place disgusting, but now I saw the immense contribution that the children had made to that house. It had never seemed like a home, but at least it had been clean and kempt.

The front door was ajar, but just as I was about to step inside, I noticed something that surprised me. A basin of a fine-looking brown stew was sitting on the front step, its cloth covering half dislodged by a scrawny-looking cat that was snatching at the meat greedily, gulping it down while keeping one eye warily on us. I stepped over the basin, disturbing the cat only as far as the edge of the step, where it hissed open-mouthed, baring its teeth. Morrie called out to me.

'Kitty, wait. Please, Kitty, you have to talk to me!' I barely heard him, but pushed the door open further and stepped inside.

The room was as dark as if it were dusk. The windows were opaque with dirt and coming from the harsh February light outside, I struggled to see. My foot touched a glass bottle that clinked against another. The flags were littered with them, most of them broken, and the wall beside the door was stained with long rivulets of watery brown stout. He must have flung each emptied bottle at the wall.

The room smelled of staleness and flatulence, and I heard his loud, fitful snoring before my eyes made him out.

He was huddled in a chair beside the hearth, which was piled with white ash in perfect imitation of turf-sods, that one touch would have evaporated. His arm cradled something that was hidden by his swollen belly, which several missing buttons showed to be pale and flaccid. The chair was surrounded with empty bottles of clear glass that bore no label.

I approached him gently, as one would a sleeping child, not wishing to wake him. The table was covered with basins similar to the one I had seen outside, and no other utensils. He must have eaten from them like the cat on the step. As I rounded the table I saw what he was cradling. Although filthy now, I recognised the long blue cashmere wrap I had sent to Veronica for her thirteenth birthday. She had worn it around her head and mouth, like a sheik of Araby.

I admit that what I most wanted to do was to clean that room while he slept, prepare some wholesome food to replace the intercepted stew and depart, leaving him ignorant of Veronica's fate. Morrie was loitering at the door, looking terrified, so I beckoned him over, consciously cruel. He was not going to escape the consequences of his actions. If Dom had been informed, he would either have refused consent and she would still be alive, or he would have agreed and the responsibility would not be ours. That was the simple equation; Veronica's death was not a factor in it.

'Dom,' I said, too softly to be effective. There was a twitching under his swollen, paper-thin eyelids, but no more. His face and eyes were puffy, whether with drink or crying or both, I couldn't tell.

'*Dom.*'

One eye opened, and the other struggled to follow, sealed with yellow matter. He seemed not to know where he was, and he looked about him in confusion. I realised that he was still quite drunk. He tried to raise himself from the chair, letting the scarf slide from him as though he had forgotten it. He gripped the arms of the chair and attempted to stand, lurching forwards, and very suddenly he stiffened, fixing his eyes on my shoes.

He stared at them for a moment, swaying slightly as he clung to the chair for support. Then with a supreme effort, he let go of the chair and thrust his hands out on either side of him, like a tightrope walker trying to balance.

His head nodded as he rose, as if the weight of it were too much for his neck. He struck a swaying pose as if he were about to dance a fluttering solo, absurdly delicate. I could not tell which of us he was looking at, for his eyes were black dots under the swollen lids. Three times he made a gutteral sound and swayed towards us, failing in his attempt to speak.

Morrie touched my hand and grimaced, indicating the door with his head, and suddenly Dom spoke, slurred but direct.

'Don't you fucking laugh at me, you mangy fucking dog,' he said, leaning too far over his feet and stumbling towards Morrie and I.

'I wouldn't laugh at you, Dom, I wouldn't do that,' said Morrie, quickly, but without retreating. Dom leaned right into him, and peered into his face, half grinning as if Morrie were a puzzle he was on the brink of solving. Morrie didn't flinch, even though the smell from his breath was suffocating even from where I was standing.

'*I've got your measure!*' he shouted triumphantly, punching his fist in the air, still grinning. Suddenly, a cloud came across his face and he breathed in and out with ever more ferocity, as if he were winding up the engine of a motor car. It was horrible to see, like the freak-show at a circus.

'*You.*' He leaned forwards, swaying wildly, as if to help him keep his head steady to fix it on Morrie.

'*You sent that skinny fuck with his bag of savagery to this house.*' I don't think he even knew I was there. He nodded vehemently, closing his eyes and revving himself up for his next announcement.

'*I had to stand with him and hear her little step THERE,*' he pointed to the ceiling above him, like a preacher, '*dressing for this fucking cur dog that filled her full of ...*'

He stopped, swaying over his centre of gravity as his eyes filled with tears.

'*Hope!*' he said suddenly, and started to swing his head from side to side, keeping time to invisible music, smiling as the pendulum rocked him back to the refrain once more: '*Hope!*'

He hung in suspension with the word for a moment, like an opera singer, and then he raised his fist to no one, shook his head violently and roared.

'*FUCKING ANIMALS!*'

Exhausted with the effort, he curled himself into a ball on the floor precise as an infant obediently taking a resented nap, and cried quietly.

We stood in silence as his grief played itself out, draining him of strength until it seemed that he could weep no more.

He was a dancing bear, the bridle cutting cruelly into his wild flesh, and it seemed that to continue to watch him was to collude in his humiliation. I picked my way through the bottles and silently began to stack the basins, emptying their rotting contents into a pail — the only clean receptacle in the house. I gathered as many bottles as I could without disturbing him and set them against the wall in the yard.

Morrie stood watching me, not daring to help.

I flung the putrid food into the pigsty, where three starving creatures fell on it and tore it apart like Dionysis. Scattered bones suggested that they had meted out the same treatment to one of their fellows.

Beside the sty I found a bucket, and I held it under the pump in the yard and cranked the handle. The rusted iron grated loudly and I froze in terror, looking to the house for fear of waking Dom, and in that moment I became, irrevocably and for an instant only, my niece.

When I ascertained that the silence continued to pour, unbroken, from the house, I heard the sounds of Shannack surge back again. The voracious pigs, the restless trees, the violent air. I made my way back into the house, passing the two of them like a ghost. I climbed the wooden stairs to her room and entered, reverentially, as if her spirit might still shyly reside there, coy of being disturbed.

It was horrifying. I could not imagine what ritual of violence had left the shattered mirror, the shredded bed linen, the burnt out basin, and by the window, a pile of cloths lay heaped up, stained with dried blood.

'O, Christ, Veronica,' I whispered, afraid almost to wake her troubled spirit. 'Tell me what to do for you, sweetheart.'

I heard noise from the room below, and I dropped to the ground, instinctively, pressing my ear to the boards. Dom had woken up. I heard him struggling to his feet, kicking bottles out of the way.

'You know what she'll look like?' I heard him say, almost conversationally.

'*Sewn up*,' he hissed, and I raced down the stairs to where he stood, squaring up to my loathsome husband, and scratching his head as if to wake himself.

He looked around him and his gaze took in the empty basins on the table as if they puzzled him. Then, all of a sudden, he shrugged his shoulders and turned back to Morrie as if something had just occurred to him.

'What do you want?' he asked.

Morrie looked over at me and said, 'Kit, wait outside.'

Dom became more alert at this, and looked at Morrie warily. I cast a cold eye over the pair of them and walked out of the front door in disgust.

The bowl was cleaned out and the cat long gone as I stepped out into the air. I walked out and stood facing the dark hedges. I closed my eyes and tried to breathe in the good, fresh air for I was feeling nauseous.

'God! That's a fierce peculiar place to take a nap, but then I suppose you're worn out from upsetting your brother-in-law,' said a voice.

My eyes opened to find a wild-haired woman looming over me. It only took a moment for me to recognise the smirking voice: Cass Carmody, Ellen's bewildering friend, was regarding me with her shrewd old eyes.

'Didn't like your bouquet, no?' she asked, shrugging her shoulders and glancing at my breast pocket. I looked down and saw the shrivelled remains of the posy of primroses I had bought from the little girl. The sight of them made something inside me snap, and I started to weep.

'Good, sweet Christ!' she said, and opened her arms to me. 'There must be something in the water round here today, I heard blubbering enough from inside in the hovel there a minute ago. Now, now. Ah here ...' and she rubbed my back awkwardly as I sobbed into her bosom.

While I cried, she kept talking to me, nonsense

mainly, about how well it was she was wearing a shawl or she'd be drowned and how the little pussy-cat wouldn't be able to stomach a mouse from this out after her good stew. Just the right things to say.

After a while, I felt well enough to be embarrassed and pulled away from her. I looked up at her but she was looking behind me, curiously. Morrie was standing in the doorway.

He didn't seem to register Cass, but spoke directly to me, his voice thick with panic.

'Kit, he hasn't moved. I told him and he hasn't moved.'

'What did you tell him?' said Cass abruptly.

Morrie turned to her, neither recognising her nor questioning who she was and said simply, 'Veronica's dead.'

Some tiny part of Cass's old face twitched and her eyes snapped shut for a second. When they opened again they were cold.

'Get back to Dublin,' she said, and she turned and walked through the door into the dark cottage.

Fourteen

I will own that I am one of those who prefer the company of adults to children. Of my own son Robert I saw relatively little when he was small, as I was doing my bit for the Empire through the Royal Army Medical Corps. When I came home on leave, I was so cynical and weary from the mutilation and the pointless suffering that a carefully regulated dose of a small boy had quite a restorative effect. It is hard to hate the world when someone is trying to put his head through his sleeve.

Grandchildren, however, are quite another matter. I have two. The twins were born just after my fall when it seemed to my family that my life was effectively over, and they were named Edward and Oliver in my honour. Their father had the good manners to marry an American woman, and so deliver us from the onerous duty of babysitting them. There were, however, The Yearly Visits. This year's visit was currently in progress, and in any other year I would have regarded it as a disaster of monumental proportions.

Robert and Eleanor had a nanny, whom they always brought with them, and the five of them would take a house in town for the month. This arrangement allowed the exhausted parents to flee to the west every so often, where Robert would fish and Eleanor, by her own admission, would sit immobile in a chair and listen to the silence.

This year, as fate would have it, the nanny was ill and Robert and Eleanor had prevailed on Alicia to take the boys for a week. She jumped at the chance, and had spent the last month buying toys and plaguing Mr Conaty with recipes to try out in anticipation of our small guests. It may be petty of me to say it, but I don't believe an elderly man should ever be forced to eat fairy buns or spotted dick. I might also add that I don't think a fine chef should be reduced to cooking them.

The timing, as it turned out, was hugely advantageous to me. The boys arrived on the Friday afternoon, and they were already ensconced when I returned from the hospital with the dreadful news. Alicia was distracted, not with grief but with trying to prevent the boys from tripping me up and knocking over the furniture.

As hard as she tried, she couldn't keep her attention on the girl's death, partly because I kept pointing in the direction of the boys' voices and making shushing sounds whenever the melancholy subject arose, and partly because the twins themselves were in perpetual, hazardous motion. Their bedtime, according to themselves, was sometime approaching midnight. That, at any rate, was the first time they showed even a sign of slowing down. I was hugely grateful for the chaos and not just because it distracted Alicia.

There had been no problem with Morrie, as it turned out. I never even gave him the option of a post-mortem, and he didn't know enough to request one. He said very little as I told him. I imagine he was looking at her and taking it in. I explained that she had died of a massive seizure, the result of an allergic reaction to the anaesthetic and that it could not have been predicted.

'Christ, Edward,' he said softly. 'Her father ...'

I suggested that he tell the man that the opportunity for surgery came up at the last minute and there was no time to send for him. I made it very clear to him, however, that that was as far as my involvement would stretch. This was a family matter.

I asked him to send my condolences to Kitty, but in deference to their sensibilities I would not linger, but leave them with their niece. I told him it would be best if he took some time alone with the girl now, as it would help him to get over the bereavement further down the line. Then he should talk to his wife while the nurse laid her out.

I found someone to take me to the records department, instructing them to take a route that did not pass Sweetman's office, and I signed her death certificate.

She went to the church on Saturday and she would be buried today, Monday, in the Bluebell cemetery in Inchicore, beside her mother. No doubt Sweetman would not like it, but short of exhuming her to tie up a loose end, there was nothing he could do about it. John Geraghty, with whom I desperately wanted to speak, had not contacted me. I suppose he must have been grieving for the girl he so strangely loved. And that was that, it was terribly sad and personally very disappointing.

I swished my drink around and let the ice clink against the glass, which apart from the ticking of the clock was the only sound in the house.

Alicia would soon be home from the cemetery, where she had insisted on going, 'to support Kitty'. Even she agreed with me that it would be inappropriate for me to attend. Or as she more bluntly put it, 'You might get lynched.'

She would be spending the rest of the day at the Halpins' home, a gathering to which I had not been invited, and, I had a shrewd suspicion, would also lack Morrie's presence. Despite appearances, the man is no fool.

The boys were in bed, and it was only seven o'clock. O thrice blessed silence! Sheila obviously knew how to deal with five-year-old American boys with no discernible boundaries, for she stood up at half past six, clapped her hands loudly and said, 'BED!'

Oliver began a pre-emptive whine (and *no* whine is as annoying as that of a small American boy) but was interrupted by the wilier Edward, whom I heard say, 'Uh, Ollie, I think this lady means business.'

And they allowed themselves to be shoo-ed upstairs, pausing only to spread mucus on their grandfather's face.

'Night, Grandpa!' they said in chorus; sweet, charming and above all, leaving.

Alicia practises little *techniques* that she picks up in women's publications, none of which have any effect save that of delaying bedtime. Last night I heard her say to Oliver, 'If you don't go to bed, you won't get all the sleep you need to grow big and strong!'

Oliver's pre-occupations were somewhat more short-term, endeavouring as he was to eviscerate Grandpa with a spoon and laughing like a criminal lunatic. Both boys find it absolutely hilarious that Grandpa is blind.

It had begun to rain again, 'sheeting down' as my mother used to say. A high wind was driving the rain against the windows in violent bursts, making me feel cold despite the fire snapping in the grate. I had felt sorry for poor Alicia, freezing in that dismal cemetery, but frankly I was glad to be indoors.

She came home soon after, her umbrella clunking into the brass stand, and she slammed open the sitting room door, banging the knob against the wall, which I cannot abide.

'Where are the boys?' she asked in a voice that shivered with cold.

'In bed, would you believe. Sheila turns out to be a natural.'

'O,' she said, a little desolately. 'I'll just go and check on them,' and she left.

Even two floors down from the boys' room I heard her bellowing, 'Boys? Are you asleep?' She got her wish and soon the three of them were scampering up and down the stairs, Alicia calling out in mock annoyance and the boys endeavouring to cave in the ceiling by jumping.

It was over an hour later that she returned, slumping into the chair opposite me in exhaustion.

'God, they're a handful,' she said with perfect sincerity and then: 'SHEILA!'

When Sheila appeared, Alicia asked her for a sherry and 'a refill for the Boss'. She must have been tired, for she never asks a servant to do something she could do herself. Sheila obliged and Alicia told her to retire for the night. I noticed that she did not thank her for taking care of the boys, as I would have expected her to do. A smile spread over my face as I realised that Sheila was being punished for out-performing Grandma.

'What?' she said, noticing it.

'Nothing,' I said, and we sat in silence for a moment.

'O, Edward, it was terrible.' She sighed, raising herself out of the chair and walking over to the drinks cabinet. She poured herself another sherry, unusually for her, and came to sit on the arm of my chair. Her free hand stroked my forehead gently, something she hasn't done for years, and she started to talk.

'I was so ashamed for you.' I made a startled sound, but she continued. 'No. Don't speak. You must hear what I have to say,' and she carried on, petting me idly.

'There was no pretence of bravery, you know? Just grief: raw, inconsolable grief. Her father was there. You never met him, did you?'

I couldn't understand how she could be so cruel. Her tone chilled me, as did the casual, gentle strumming of her hand on my face.

'No. That's right, you didn't. He's a big man, really. Florid looking and I would think quite shy. Not a person who would be comfortable being the centre of attention, I shouldn't imagine. But he was. Everyone was looking at him. Even I couldn't take my eyes off him when her coffin came in. Such a small coffin; plain deal, nothing elaborate. Made me think perhaps that he had paid for it himself, that perhaps he wasn't so keen that Morrie Halpin would be the person to have control over how she was ... presented, shall we say?'

'Stop, Alicia. Please.'

'No, I think I will continue.' She said mildly, and moved her gentle hands to my pate. 'He coughed a lot. I thought it was coughing, anyway. Turns out they were sobs, but he was trying very hard to disguise them, in the church, at any rate. I think he had washed his face that morning, because it was a completely dif-ferent colour to his neck and it made a tide-line. He wore a suit, too. I imagine it was a mark of respect.' She paused, and I prayed to God that she would stop, but she did not. Her voice was still soft.

'He was very dignified, all things considered. Yes. I quite admired him, although my heart broke for him. It was when they lowered her into the earth that he snapped.'

She stopped again, softly running her hands over my head as the rain flung itself violently against the window. I don't think I have ever been so frightened.

'I don't think you ever met Ellen, did you?'

She laughed, girlishly, a sound made grotesque by the crack of age in her voice.

'No, of course you didn't, what am I thinking of? Kitty says she was really quite special. And that she loved him. It must be true, mustn't it? Because Kitty hated him and she would hardly have gifted him his wife's love if it wasn't true, now would she? The rain was terrible by then, but of course, you can hear it now. It was just like this. The grave-diggers were slipping at the edges as they tried to lower her down into her mother's grave. It was quite labour intensive, actually.'

'Alicia,' I pleaded, 'please stop.'

'Well, I'm nearly done anyway. It doesn't take long to tell the rest.'

Her hand stilled and she rested it on my cheek, still gently.

'He threw himself down on the earth and leaned far into the open grave and howled out: "*Ellen!*" as if she were in danger and he could not reach her. Then he cried out again and again, as if he were trying to make her hear him: "*I'm so sorry! I'm so sorry! I'm so sorry! Ellen, I'm so sorry! I'm so sorry! I'm so sorry! I'm so sorry! I'm so sorry! Ellen, I'm so sorry!*"'

'NO!' I shouted, and wrenched my face away from her tightening grip. I placed my head in my hands and rocked back and forth, trying to loosen the image from my mind. She sat on the arm of the chair and didn't touch me.

'Edward,' she said, calmly. 'I tell you all this so that you will understand something. I promised to be yours until death, and now that you are blind and helpless I will never desert you, but I must tell you that unfortunately I have discovered that ...'

She stopped, conscious of the irrevocability of what she was about to say.

'I do not love you. I am so afraid that henceforth I will resent every assistance I give you, and I will hate you for your helplessness. It is intolerable, I know, and I am sorrier for it than I can ever express to you—'

Her voice clouded over with tears and she came around the chair and knelt before me, and I heard her old knees crunch with the effort. She took my face in her hands and I knew that she was looking into my miserable eyes.

'But that is just the way it is,' she said, almost in a whisper, choked and resolute.

A single tear rolled down my cheek, and I searched inside myself for something to say to her, curious almost to know how I felt.

'I understand,' I said, and I did. She straightened up, walked out of the room and closed the door.

After she had gone, an overwhelming emotion flooded into me.

It was relief: relief that I had married a woman so fine and truthful, relief that we had undertaken the marriage vows, that she could not leave me.

Fifteen

I thought I had escaped, ducking under the wisteria into the summerhouse, clutching a glass of cloudy lemonade like a stolen loaf, and for a few blessed, blessed moments I was alone. I brushed the leaves and fallen flowers from the wicker chair and sat down, holding the cold glass to my burning cheeks, too tired even to physicalise the smile I wore on the inside.

I had nagged Morrie for months to have the gardeners deal with the little pergola, complaining that it was beginning to look like a tree, but he ignored me, as usual.

Thank God. Now I drank the lemonade behind its dappled drapes gratefully, or rather my tongue soaked it up like a sponge before it had time to trickle down my throat.

In another instance of 'be careful what you wish for' I had prayed that the fifth of June would be a sunny day, in contrast to the relentlessly soggy May we had endured. It seemed that whole month passed indoors, trying to keep Corina amused and watching the common cold make a closed loop around the household. Me, Corina, Morrie, Mrs Scallon, Peggy, Jean, me, Corina, etc.

The first and the second were encouragingly dry, and I was emboldened to race into town to buy a canvas paddling pool – since the pond was now filled with Morrie's Koi – and two extra foxford rugs. Morrie had ordered a wonderful hammock to be shipped over from Hamley's, decorated as a ship under full sail, really a beautiful thing although I'm sure the shipping clerk would have assumed it a present for a son rather than a daughter.

Passing 'The Fanciers Stores' on Ormond Quay on the third, I chanced to see a quite enormous blue and yellow macaw in a gilt cage, obviously screeching its head off although, separated from me by glass, it looked as if it was gurning. What madness possessed me to buy it I'll never know, but there I was, ten minutes later sitting at Nelson's Pillar on the 14 tram for Rathmines, miserably trying to hold the vast cage of yowling bird aloft while the conductor attempted to switch the seat-backs. Heads did not so much turn as stay rigidly fixed on me, glaring. I was already mortified by my purchase.

I'm pretty sure the logic that underlay it went thus: despite my best efforts, my soon-to-be-five daughter was a tomboy. Therefore if my husband insisted on buying her a ship, I would facilitate her becoming a pirate.

Or more truthfully: if the hammock is from Morrie, I would like to get her something else.

Corina was enchanted by both presents, which was all that mattered, really. She immediately named the macaw 'Gillian', because our neighbours' twelve-year-old daughter happened to be in her eye-line at the time, and by the time I tiptoed away from the party with my sneaky lemonade, he had been by turns 'Mr Blue', 'Ship', 'Pieces' (an imperfectly heard adult suggestion: 'Pieces of Eight'), 'That bloody bird' (a perfectly overheard suggestion of Alicia Coote's) and the hasty replacement suggestion lest the last should stick: 'Screechy.'

This one did stick, drawing as it did the squealed approval of Corina's *seventeen* small guests: yes, apart from the children of actual relatives and friends, I had lovingly and of my own volition written out twelve invitations for Corina's entire kindergarten class, regardless of the fact that only a few of them were her friends: was I actually insane?

So I lolled in the wicker chair in the shade, and listened to the sounds of my daughter's party guests recede. I had not expected so many of the little darlings' parents to flee, forgoing the champagne and canapés I had carefully laid on as bait, preferring, perhaps, to lie in the quiet shade as I was.

I could not stay long at any rate, for the fragile house of cards out there was being held together by only four and two half-adults, Peggy, Jean, next-door's Olivia Brady, Alicia Coote and her eleven-year-old American grand-twins Eddie and Ollie. Gorgeous, handsome, ridiculously tall, tan lads, but quiet and slightly bewildered by the mutinous little girls swooping between ship and shore, making beloved dolls walk the plank for relatively minor offences.

I heard a step, a cautious step, that hesitated behind the curtain of wisteria, wondering whether to enter. It sounded like a little person's step.

'Come i-in!' I sang wearily, resigned to having been found out.

Gravely, through the pale fronds of foaming flowers, stepped Screechy. He cocked his head to one side, as if to wonder would I be inclined to make as much noise as the other bipeds he had met today, flapped in one violent movement onto the back of the only available chair, closed his eyes and snuggled shudderingly into his own neck.

I held my hand over my mouth and broke up laughing as silently as I could, for his demeanour so accurately mirrored my own. Perhaps I would not be bringing him back to the shop as soon as Corina tired of him, as I had promised my husband.

'Mummy! Mummy!' Speak of angels, there she was, calling in the wrong part of the garden for her deserter mother. I couldn't hide any longer.

'I'm in here, darling!' I called, earning a withering look from Screechy.

Corina burst through the wisteria. Flowers fell around her like confetti and she appeared as always: edibly pretty and surrounded by falling or breaking things.

'Mummy! I can't find Screechy! O!' This last exclamation as she spotted Screechy jumping lumpenly to the floor, not much aided by his out-stretched wings and stalking out in exasperation.

'Mummy! Mummy!' On to the next topic she went without skipping a beat. 'Daddy and Uncle John are back, and they've got Luke with them!'

'Lovely, darling,' I said, relieved to have some adult reinforcement. 'Where are they?'

A shadow rose up behind her and the foliage, and a familiar voice said, 'Funny you should ask!' and in came John Geraghty and his six-month-old son, Luke, dressed so frilly and flouncy that he could have been his daughter.

'Clever you,' he said, looking around the shady little pergola admiringly. 'A cool haven from the madness without.'

'Uncle John and Luke got me a book, Mummy!' Corina squeaked. 'But I have it already,' she said in a matter of fact way, as if it was a slightly disappointing fact that needed to be acknowledged but not dwelt on.

'Corina!' I said, mortified, but John waved his free hand and said, 'I already explained to Corina that it was Luke who chose it, so she'll have to have it out with him in a year or so when he can talk.'

'And I will!' said she in a bold-as-brass voice that made me fear the party was going to have to end in a smacking and sending to bed. Not that! Please God, no!

'Run away back to the ship, little woman, and see if you can round up those mutineers,' I said, hoping that she might expend some of the naughtiness there, for I could not be expected to punish crimes I did not witness.

'Aye aye, Mummy!' she said, and saluted as she ripped through the wisteria.

As the petals settled around him, I thought how fine a man John Geraghty had turned out to be. After all the pain of five years ago, he disappeared from our lives, and indeed he almost disappeared full stop. I think he blamed himself, and I'm sure he felt that we blamed him. Morrie came across him just over two years ago. Perhaps it had taken him that long to forgive himself.

Morrie, who forgave himself almost instantly, had immediately set up a charity to fund research into allergic reactions such as the one that killed our niece. Two years ago John Geraghty applied for the newly vacant post of director of the Veronica Trust, an unpaid but time-consuming post. My husband was favourably impressed, and not long after, he and his wife came to a dinner at our new house in Rathmines to formally welcome him to the position, and more pertinently, back into our lives.

He was a newlywed at that time, and when I saw him that first evening, I was struck by how fantastically *healthy* he looked! He had filled out pleasantly — the result of Beth's good cooking, he assured us — and his high colour was replaced by a golden tan.

Beth was from Killiney village, and had persuaded her new husband to take up a practice in her home-place. There the two of them worked up an appetite each evening by walking their dogs for miles along the shore. Beth was a former nurse — although she had retired upon marriage, of course — and she was lovely.

Teeny-tiny, like a rosy-cheeked boy, she looked up while her husband spoke, like a geisha.

Later that night, Beth turned her gentle attentiveness to Morrie, who was only too delighted to have someone to listen to him with an unjaundiced ear, and I was left to talk to John.

We talked of Veronica. The subject had lain between my husband and I for so many years like a sword, and it was like a release of pressure to just chat about her once more. We didn't analyse events, or even dwell on her death, we just talked about the girl we had known.

Only once did we both come close to tears. Looking up at John, self-assured and relaxed, lighting a cigar from a candle, I said to him, 'I think she was in love with you.'

He stopped, and looked at me, and our eyes filled at the same instant and he said quietly, 'I think she was, just a little bit.'

We sat in silence for a while, companionably, thinking about our poor little friend, and then we spoke of other things.

✿

Luke grizzled and squirmed, his face suddenly turning bright red in the way of infants, and much as his father had done in the old days.

'Uh-oh,' he said, 'I knew that wouldn't last long, this is about as long as he's ever been away from his mummy!' Luke flung his head back and made an exploratory 'Waah!'

'I can't tell you how good it was of Morrie to come and get me. Beth thinks he's a kind of demigod, by the way.'

Beth was with child again, and Morrie had conceived a clever plan to miss most of the party, gain a male companion *and* have everyone think he was the kindest man on earth. It was a consummate skill, and about the only thing about him that I still grudgingly admired.

'Here,' I said, reaching over for the ticking bomb that was Luke. 'Leave him here in the shade and send Jean to me, Corina's nanny? She can take him for a bit, and you and Morrie can find a dark nook to drink beer in.' John grinned over to me and got to his feet.

'You're wonderful, Kitty.' And he stooped under the wisteria.

'O,' he said, hesitating in the portal. 'Two things. First, he's just been fed, so it's not that.'

'Ah, marvellous,' I said, turning Luke upside down to have a sniff.

'And second ... was that Mrs Coote I saw up at the house?'

'Yes,' I replied, 'and she still hates you if that's what you're wondering. I mentioned you were coming and she said, "O, goody," in *that* voice, but don't fret, the worst she'll do is look at you like you're dirt.'

'O, goody,' said John grimly, and left.

John had correctly diagnosed Luke's problem, and the little pergola became progressively less and less pleasant as I waited for Jean to extract herself from the party and deal with him.

✿

By six o'clock, we were entering the danger zone. Corina was very put out not to have Jean, her personal slave and attendant, hovering perpetually in her immediate vicinity ready to fulfil her every whim. Jean was under instructions to let discipline lapse for the day, and in only eight hours Corina had adapted to the new arrangement like a natural, barking orders or starting a sentence randomly with, 'I want aaaaaaaa …' sensing that, for this day only, everyone would have to wait patiently to find out what she would decide to want.

The party was winding down, and, by my last head count, we were down to four non-domestic, non-family interlopers.

John had just emerged from Morrie's study, presumably leaving my husband bereft, and volunteered to take over Jean's duties with Corina, which was only fair, but he could easily have dodged it.

He was fully engrossed in a game of wizard doctor, by which he enquired the symptoms of Corina's terrible illness. Was her skin blue or green? Blue! Hee-hee-hee! Had she any unusual objects growing out of her that weren't there yesterday? A cat! Ha-ha-ha! It was a difficult case. If only someone could tell him if she needed the castor-oil pill or the chocolate-fudge pill. I know! I know!

It was as well he was preoccupied, for Alicia and the boys were making their way over to me to say their goodbyes. I steered them discreetly out into the hall, and accepted the boys' solemn thankyous for a swell time. Ma'am.

Alicia looked tired as she offered her cheek to me for a kiss.

'Give my best to Edward,' I said with a concerned look, which we both understood.

Edward was much altered. He had aged beyond belief in the last five years, the spark in him irrevocably gone. I visited them little, I confess, both Alicia and I seeming to prefer to meet in Rathmines.

He did nothing for himself now, letting Alicia care for him as if he were a baby. In the last year he became, for some reason I didn't fully understand, unable to use the bathroom, and Alicia changed him, always uncomplaining, although she was no longer young herself. He had become that thing which every older person fears: a burden, though it seemed that his failing faculties did not allow him to feel shame, perhaps a mercy: he seemed quite content with his lot.

Alicia became almost businesslike about her responsibility to Edward, and seized every opportunity that presented itself to pursue her own pleasures. She would make him comfortable, see her many friends, and be home in time to cater to his regimented needs. It was sad to see, for they had been an old age that I had used as a role model for Morrie and I in simpler times.

'Take care of that hellion daughter of yours,' she said, the old glint appearing briefly in her grey eyes.

'I will,' I said. 'Take care of those fine men, and make sure they come back to Ireland when my Corina is old enough to appreciate them!'

Eddie blushed scarlet and looked at his shoes at exactly the same moment that Ollie burst out enthusiastically, 'Yes, ma'am!'

Perhaps they were not so alike after all.

I waved them all off, and by my previous headcount, the interlopers were down to two.

Two separate collectors of children were making their way up the drive – hurrah! – a man and a woman. I recognised both of them vaguely. One, I thought, was Holly Renmore's father (when *could* her birthday be?) whom I often saw going in and out of the town hall in Rathmines, so a civil servant of some kind, but what name? The woman was maddeningly familiar, but I couldn't place her. However, by process of elimination she was Cassie Keane's mother.

Liam Renmore did the maddening thing of offering his hand and saying 'Liam Renmore' just as I remembered that his name was Liam Renmore, thereby depriving me of the opportunity of appearing omniscient. I remembered, though, that he was, in fact, the assistant Dublin City Manager, so I assured him that he 'must meet my husband,' and hustled him into the study where Morrie, I had no doubt, would quickly persuade him to grant us permission to build the sun-parlour I had dreamed of for the past three years.

'You're very welcome, Mrs Keane,' I said, offering my hand. 'Cassie has been an absolute delight.' A quiet child, she had not registered with me until she had become one of the last to leave, lingering forlornly on the hammock after all the buccaneering had long ceased.

Corina skidded through the hallway, squealing and rucking the Persian runner, closely pursued by John, who yelled, 'Take your medicine! The cat said syrup of figs!'

I turned around, laughing apologetically, to find Mrs Keane staring beyond me, frozen almost.

'I'm sorry about that,' I said gently. 'It's a bit of a boisterous house today, I'm afraid.'

She looked at me with a most peculiar expression and then smiled stiffly. 'No, no,' she said, quietly.

I retreated into the garden and retrieved the melancholy Cassie, concerned for her slightly, but relieved to see them go.

❁

By nine, the house was quiet. Morrie had taken John and Luke home, the last, forgotten interloper, and Corina had finally admitted defeat and had agreed to go – not to bed, precisely – but to sleep on the high seas cuddled up in eiderdowns with Jean on the hammock.

I had just settled in the parlour, sipping a sherry and fondly looking out at them, when Peggy came in.

'Mrs Halpin, there's a lady to see you.' I had not heard the bell.

'Do we know her, Peggy?' I asked, a little bewildered.

'Mrs Keane?' she said, with an 'I'm none the wiser either' look on her face.

'Em, send her in, thanks, Peg.'

Peggy led her into the room, and that nagging familiarity attended her once more. She stood in the doorway, uncertainly, and looked apologetic.

'Come in, Mrs Keane,' I said, 'How lovely to see you again so soon.'

She winced, and I felt embarrassed by my clumsiness.

'Sit down, won't you?'

She did, and removed her hatpin and her hat slowly, placing them on a side table.

'Mrs Halpin,' she said, and I instantly recognised her, the click and whistle over the back teeth on the letter 's', the kindly face drained of light-heartedness.

I stared at her as though she were a ghost. There was no need to tell her that I recognised her, for it was written all over my face. I felt precisely as I had in Reggie Sweetman's study, transfixed by her, knowing she portended ill and needing to hear it.

'I'm sorry, Mrs Halpin. I know I'm just bringing dreadful memories back to you. I've actually done everything I could to keep out of your way, since I found out that your Corina was in Cassie's class, but today, with what I saw...'

She looked at me, and I felt somehow I should know what she meant. Something clicked in the back of my mind.

'John Geraghty?' I said. What a strange momentary confluence had happened in that hall. Veronica's aunt, Veronica's nurse, Veronica's doctor. Veronica's cousin too, if she had only lived to see it.

'Yes. I had no idea you continued to see him,' she said simply.

'Only in the last few years,' I said, knowing that it was none of her business, but strangely not feeling offended. There was obviously something she needed to say to me.

'My mother told me to keep it to myself. She agonised about it for days, and said she couldn't see what good it would do. Let the dead rest, is what she said.'

'Your mother?' I said, bewildered by the turn the conversation had taken.

'O, I'm sorry, I thought you knew. I'm Cass Carmody's daughter. I saw you at Liam's wedding, but perhaps you didn't see me.'

A dark-coated shape beside her flamboyant mother, I remembered.

'Mrs Keane, what have you to tell me? I can see that something concerns you about Dr Geraghty, but you haven't said what, and to be honest you're quite chilling me.'

'I'm so sorry, Mrs Halpin. I would never have given you this if I hadn't seen him there, so happy playing with your daughter. If it were me I would want to know, seeing that he is back in your life.' And she reached over to the side table, picked up her handbag and extracted a weathered white envelope, which she laid on the table. Then she picked up her hat and put it on, taking her time to insert the hatpin, as if she were still thinking. She stood up. I went to rise, but she stopped me with a hand gesture.

'No, I'll let myself out, thank you. I'll leave you to read that at your leisure. Mrs Halpin . . .'

She seemed reluctant to continue, as if she were fearful of overstepping some boundary.

'Yes,' I said, my heart pounding.

'When you read it, Mrs Halpin, you must understand that it is not just the note itself. It is what I *saw*. I saw his face when he read it, and it was what I saw there that made me pick it up where he threw it. It's not a thing I'd normally do, you must understand. You have to know that I have never seen that look in any person before. I will never forget it as long as I live, it *frightened* me, Mrs Halpin.'

She lowered her head then, as if she had said more than she intended to, took her handbag up from the chair, and left the room.

I sat for a moment, feeling the hairs rising on my neck. I looked out the window to my beautiful Corina, nestled amongst nanny and eiderdown, rocking to sleep in a ship in full sail in the moonlight.

I reached over and picked up the envelope. It was not sealed. I drew out the yellowing torn page, folded in two, and I opened it.

My heart lurched as I recognised her careful handwriting, neat and tidy, following an invisible margin and signed as formally as a clerk.

Dear Dr Geraghty

Thank you for what you said about loving me utterly and wanting me to be yours forever. It was very nice to hear it and it made me forget all about being nervous.

I don't think I should say yes because after you make my mouth beautiful I might have much more choice.

Yours truly
Veronica Broderick

Five,

Four,

Three …

I'm so glad I learned about the game. If I didn't know anything about it I'd be in the wrong story, taking on my prince when I'm still ugly. Now I can make the story just right *and* I am dangling him on a thread, just the way Kitty does Morrie. I will wake up beautiful and say, 'Yes, Dr Geraghty, I will marry you.' And the story will be happy ever after.

I am toying with a lover.

I am a woman.

Acknowledgments

So many people have helped in one way or another with the making of this book, but I would like to thank these people in particular.

Dearbhle and Morna Regan and Michael Scott for their early encouragement and help. The early readers and encouragers, Cathy Belton, Fiona Bell, Emma Colohan, Paul Meade, Colm Tóibín and Eugene O'Brien.

Kevin Parsons and Claire Sweeney for making a quiet, windswept haven in Mayo available to me whenever I needed it, and the guardians and 'housemates' at Annaghmakerrig.

Andy Harkin for removing the barriers.

Joan Ardiff, for putting a smile on my face, and all my friends and relatives who made me feel like it wasn't a silly notion to write a book.

All at New Island, especially Deirdre Nolan and Thomas Cooney for their unflagging support. Fidelma Slattery for her beautiful design.

Ger Nichol at The Book Bureau agency for being a true enabler and encourager. Every writer should have an agent like her.

And Aisling Ardiff. She falls into all the categories above, having provided editing, agency, friendship, encouragement and wisdom.

Finally, fifteen years ago my Dad bought me a computer. It was a Schneider Euro PC and the screen was black with orange writing on it. He typed the first sentence on it: 'This is the computer on which Karen will write her first novel.' Well, it took me a long time and he will have to read it in astral form, but I don't think he necessarily wanted to read it. He just wanted me to write it.